Eilwen

This book is dedicated to my grandpa, Alvin William Wicke, my grandma, Mary Alice Wicke, my granduncle, Robert Louis Wicke, and to the beautiful state of Kentucky.

Acknowledgments:

I would like to thank Natalie Wicke, the best friend and cousin anyone could ever ask for, for being the first person I let read this book and for being nothing but encouraging.

Table of Contents:

Chapter I

Knack for Planting

Tobacco's but an Indian weed,
Grows green at morn, cut down at eve;
It shows decay; we are but clay;
Think of this when you smoke tobacco.
– George Wither, "Tobacco"

The dead snake stared up at them, unblinking. Snakes cannot blink, however, so aside from the fact that its stomach was trampled, it could have appeared alive.

"Would you like to say a few words?"

Eilwen Tabb looked at her little brother, Gus, who was poised to sprinkle dirt over the grave. It had been easy to dig, being so near the creek.

He sighed, then nodded with the dramatic solemnity of his six years. "Hail Mary, full of grace, the –"

Eilwen smacked the back of his head. "Not *those* words." Gus snorted at her. "You want me to tell Aunt you were down here by the crick muttering Catholic verses like that?"

"Marcy taught me that prayer at school!"

"Marcy's a papist. Aunt don't like you talking to her."

"*You* say a few words!" Gus threw the dirt in his hand at Eilwen.

Eilwen stuck her tongue out at him as she wiped it off. Not that it made much difference: her shirt was soiled and sweaty from three straight days of plowing fields. She shook her stray hairs out of her face, crossed her hands in

1

front of her and cleared her throat. "We are here today to honor the life of this poor, dear snake, tragically cut down —"

"What's 'tragically' mean?" asked Gus.

"Really sad," said Eilwen. "Tragically cut down in her prime by —"

"How do you know it's a girl snake?"

"How do you know it's not? Tragically cut down in…" she paused, waiting for Gus to interrupt again, then continued, "in her prime by the swift and sharp prejudice that so frequently befalls her kind."

"I thought Mahitabel trampled it to death."

"I was trying to say it more proper than just spittin' it out plain like that, but… yes." Eilwen bowed her head. Gus did the same. "Rest in peace, snakey. Thank you for keeping our barn clean of rats as long as you did. May the rest of your kind stay away from horses. Amen."

"Amen," Gus echoed. He grabbed another handful of dirt and tossed it on the grave.

Eilwen and her brother worked together to bury the snake completely. Soon the black racer's sleek scales, smooth to sight and touch, vanished beneath brown clods of earth.

Morning sun crept through the green-speckled bracken. The creek began to sparkle. Eilwen and Gus trudged back up the wooded slope toward the Homestead, the mist of early morning that gathered in the hilly countryside's countless valleys seeming to burn away before their eyes. The air, still crisp, gained a sweeter taste. Eilwen had to stop and savor it for a few breaths.

Gus continued lolloping ahead.

2

Waking up to snake cadavers in horse stalls was a sure sign of spring, if nothing else. The snakes, stirring from hibernation in the hay, venture forth for their first meal in months, only to discover skittish equines, whose first impulse upon serpent sighting is to trample. It was an unavoidable evil; farmers were always loath to see a good snake go to waste. They were the ultimate pest control. But for young Eilwen, who felt an innate kinship with the misunderstood and the pointlessly trampled, the pain of seeing a dead snake ran deeper.

Shep barked as Eilwen and Gus neared the Homestead: a log cabin it was said Thomas Lincoln had helped construct back before Kentucky had even become a state. The sheepdog ran to greet them, then hurried back to the porch, where he lay down by an empty rocking chair. Eilwen looked around, but saw no one. She tried to push her worried feeling aside, however. There was nothing unusual about an empty rocker. It had been empty in the mornings for days now, and that had meant nothing bad so far.

Eilwen kissed Gus goodbye for the day and took off.

Cows mooed as Eilwen jogged past the grazing fields and headed for the tobacco fields past the curing barn. Little Gus stayed by the house, where he was to be of whatever assistance he could tending the seedlings with their granduncle. But nine-year-old Eilwen was to pull her weight – and then some – plowing from dawn until dusk. Aunt Mona and Uncle Dale were already in the fields, and had been since breakfast. Eilwen and Gus had been doing the year-round morning chores around the farm for the past few hours, saving their unanticipated snake funeral for the last minute.

Eilwen was glad to be made to use the handplow for once. She was still sore at Mahitabel for her thoughtless killing, and didn't think she'd be able to civilly work a plow with her.

* * *

Every so often, an urge strikes those who have just seen the face of their newborn child: an urge to bestow upon the child a name as unusual as the urge itself. Why the child in question should warrant a unique name is a mystery. After all, the babe appears no different physically, or behaviorally, from any other. Yet still there remain, as there have throughout history, those select introductions wherein a parent sees their child, stops suddenly and thinks, "A common name just won't do."

Such a thought had never occurred to Mona Hittle, who, having struggled with circumstances of which society is entirely expectant yet never accepting, once tried rip a child from her birth name.

When Mona had first butted heads with the then three-year-old Eilwen Tabb, it had seemed a prelude of conflict to come that their clash should concern the child's name – her identity.

"She'll respond to nothing else," Eilwen's previous caretaker had warned Mona. "Stubborn tot."

But Mona, just as stubborn as her toddling adversary, had ignored the warning. Every child could be broken. And hard-headed Eilwen, with her flashy eyes and lurid name, was in need.

But the warning had held true.

For the first couple years after bringing Eilwen to her new home at the Hittles' farmstead, Mona had dubbed her Eileen, Ellen, Elaine, and Margaret. None of which Eilwen had responded to, and, to Mona's shock, none of which any amount of beating could make her.

Every piece of literature named her Eileen. Every document – even the 1930 census record – listed Eileen Margaret Tabb as the sole female child resident of the Hittle household on Bloomfield Road in Bardstown, Kentucky. Eilwen, as far as the law was concerned, did not exist. Eilwen had not even existed as far as Mona was concerned until she had been seven years old, by which time Mona had grown weary of the fight.

Eilwen herself had never understood why she clung to her name. It was just a word, after all. The older she got, the more aware she became that she had been alone in the self-awareness she'd possessed at so young an age. All she knew for certain was that some nights, while she slept, a voice in the furthest recesses of her mind reminded her: "Eilwen. Your name is Eilwen."

The voice was faded, and over the years Eilwen worried she would forget it, but it had remained with her: the words clear, the tone urgent – almost pleading. Eilwen wondered who must have said this to her. The voice was a woman's, but it couldn't have been her mother's. Eilwen's mother had been too busy keeping her husband from the bottle to say two words to her children.

"Not that her first-born would've been worth talking to," Mona liked to remind her niece. And Eilwen, embarrassed of the disgrace she brought her family, would look away in shame.

It was unforgiveable to have a child out of wedlock. The best salve for such social scars was for the community to let the family cover up as best they could, then never speak of it again.

What was even more unforgiveable, however, was when a family did nothing to hide it. Mona's tramp of a sister had not even attempted to cover up the illegitimate birth of Eilwen, which had made the family's recovery – or lack thereof – all the worse.

"So my sister ran away to Bowling Green with that drunk father of yours, married the bastard to save face, and died giving life to your brother," was what Eilwen had been told for as long as she could remember. "A mercy killing if there ever was one. Your father's likely dead too. Haven't seen or heard from him since the day I brought you and Gus to live here. Good riddance!"

Eilwen rarely endeavored to slight her aunt Mona, but by the time she'd turned nine, she'd accepted it was inevitable. Eilwen's very existence was a slight. She was a bastard. Her brother, despite killing their mother, was an angel, with the impenetrable shield of having been born in wedlock. Eilwen could do no right, and she had learned to accept this. She had grown to expect punishment at every turn.

It was even more difficult when – on top of being a bastard – you were so very easily distracted. Every time Eilwen grew brave enough to think herself a good worker, she would find herself yanked by the hair, locked in the cellar, beaten, or whipped – sometimes all four. All for "slacking off." She had a tendency to pause suddenly and stair off into the distance – to savor the air she breathed. To gaze wistfully across the green hills and ancient forests on the boundaries of the fields, her attention snared by the breeze on her cheek, or the wind lifting her hair…

But distraction was not to be tolerated. Least of all from Eilwen. Time spent daydreaming was time the cows could have spent getting milked, or soil could have spent being fertilized. And did Eilwen have any idea how much damage a hornworm could inflict on a single tobacco plant in the minute she'd just wasted staring at clouds? God help her, she was useless!

Why, Eilwen ought to be grateful anyone had taken her in after her mother died! Only out of the goodness of Mona's heart did her niece and nephew have a roof over their heads – the roof of a house, and not an orphanage. And thank heavens: while August Henry, blue-eyed and well-named, might have found a home with decent folks, no family would have adopted Eilwen. Not with her name. Not with her swarthy face. And certainly not with her sickly yellow eyes. Sick children were risky – no one could afford to waste food on lost causes. Folks were scrambling over each other as it was to dump their kids in orphanages in the wake of the Depression, yet saintly Mona had rescued both Gus *and* Eilwen from that fate. And she, too, scarcely able to afford it!

"I can still barely afford it, you parasite! As little work as you do around here!" Mona screeched late that afternoon, heaving and sweaty. The sun was low; tree shadows striped the hills, stretching from the groves that divided the fields. "How about I hitch you to the plow? Maybe that'll teach you to pull your weight!"

Her hand cracked across Eilwen's face.

Eilwen stumbled sideways. Mona unhitched Mabel, the mule, from the plow she'd been working, while Uncle Dale unhitched Mahitabel from his. They both began leading their animals back across the field toward the barn. "You can come eat supper when you've done as much work as the rest of us!" Mona screamed over her shoulder.

Eilwen dared not even rub her cheek until Mona was out of sight. Then, bolstered by the knowledge that Mona could not deny her food for long if she expected her to be of any help tomorrow, she took up the handplow and set back to work.

Five fields needed plowing before the week's end. The seedlings were ripening and the weather was turning. And Old Hal – Uncle Dale's father, patriarch of the Homestead – would be of little use this year. His eighth decade was finally revealing in him some age-related ware, enough that even Mona agreed the taxing task of tobacco tending was too much for him this season. The old man huffed simply climbing the stairs these days. "Pity we can't shoot him," Mona had muttered earlier that week, while performing her after-supper sewing by the heat-stove. "Any other animal loses usefulness around here gets shot. People should be no different." Her stare had lingered on Eilwen.

Stars stared down at Eilwen now. Sweat dripped from her chin as the iron plow fought her shaky steps. She cursed herself for slipping up – for pausing to stare at the trees across the field. The forest began there, behind the oak on the hill beside the curing barn. There was an

8

alluring quality to those trees – to the woods where bootleggers abounded, and perhaps even fairies dwelled. She had only meant to glance. Mona wasn't supposed to have seen. But Mona spent as much time watching Eilwen as she did work herself.

It was entirely dark when Eilwen, passed out at a stationary plow, felt a hand on her shoulder. She gasped and flinched – Mona was steadying her for another smack...

But no pain came.

Instead, a gentle voice said, "Come inside, now, Eilwen. It's too dark to see."

The smell hit her then: pipe tobacco. Warm, thick, heady. That smell and that voice would be forever intertwined in her mind – impossible to sense one without imagining the other. The sound and smell of her only friend in the world.

Eilwen nodded mindlessly and turned toward Old Hal.

"Come on, missy," Hal said with a grunt as he scooped Eilwen into his arms. He carried her piggy-back across the fields, huffing from strain, but never faltering. Only then did exhaustion ache through Eilwen's previously numb body. She was hungry enough to heave, but had nothing to throw up. She buried her face in the back of Hal's shirt.

Soon Hal was puffing up the stone steps of the side porch. The hand-hewn cabin loomed against the starry sky, and soon Eilwen was inside. She barely felt Hal set her on the floor. She didn't realize until too late that he had gone, struggling up the stairs in the front hall.

"I suppose you left the plow in the field?"

Mona was suddenly in front of Eilwen.

9

"Just left it out there for any wandering thief to –"

"I'm sorry."

Smack!

"Don't interrupt! Eat and get to bed! God, you're filthy! First thing tomorrow, you're doing laundry. Though there's no getting rid of your stench. What are you waiting for? Whatever you've not eaten in two minutes, I'm throwing to the hog!"

Eilwen inhaled what leftovers she could in the time allotted, then stumbled up the narrow stairs in the back of the kitchen. She was thrilled for once at the sight of her bed in the far corner of the dark upstairs.

For three years, Eilwen's bed had been a rectangular pile of straw with a quilt. Sheets sometimes, if Mona felt gracious. When Eilwen and Gus had first arrived six years ago, Eilwen had had a bed of her own, but the privilege had been revoked after she had wet it too many times. Eilwen had asked Mona recently if, since her last accident had been over two years ago, she might have a mattress again, but apparently it could not be risked. Eilwen had even lied, telling Mona she had stopped having the nightmares that had first led to her accidents. But Mona either hadn't believed her or hadn't cared.

Gus was asleep on his bed in the adjacent corner. He and Eilwen shared a spacious room that was nearly half the upper story. It had been built as slave quarters, added to the original cabin – along with the kitchen, living room and dining room – long before the Civil War. That was what Old Hal said. Hal's father had fought in the war. Hal's grandfather had commissioned the additions. The flooring – like the rest of the house – was thick slabs of

10

poplar, smooth from a century of foot traffic. The wall that had been the back of the original cabin held a window that had been boarded to prevent slaves looking in on their masters. Today, the masters' quarters belonged to Aunt Mona and Uncle Dale, and apart from breaking through the boards, there was no way to access the grownups' half of the upstairs from Eilwen and Gus's half. The grownups had their own staircase in the front of the house; the claustrophobic slave stairs behind the kitchen were for the children.

Though tired, Eilwen tiptoed over to Gus and waved a hand in front of him. Satisfied he was asleep, she returned to her bed, lit the candle on the stool beside it, and quietly dug through the straw beneath her pillow. She recovered – with reverent delicateness – an old lidded can. The ancient peanut butter label was faded and ripped, but Eilwen popped off the lid with so bright a face one would have thought there was gold inside.

And gold there was.

Eilwen pulled from the can a pure gold pocket watch. A long gold chain trailed glisteningly after.

She held the watch, watching it twinkle in the candlelight. She coiled the chain around her finger to keep it from clinking against the can, then leaned back on her pillow, clicked the hunter-case open, and relaxed, watching the secondhand tick.

It was Hal's watch. And a secret Eilwen must take to her grave. Uncle Dale had grown up expecting to inherit the watch that had survived civil war and the tumultuous decades following. None could ever know Hal had slipped the watch to Eilwen last month as a birthday treat for turning nine. He'd sworn Eilwen to secrecy – told her goblins would get her if she told anyone. Eilwen never knew how serious he was being when he said things like that, though she'd never dream of betraying him.

When five minutes had passed, Eilwen sighed and clicked the watch shut. She placed it back in the can (which also held an arrowhead, a tin soldier, and some cotton she'd found to cushion the watch). Once everything was safe beneath the straw, she covered it with her pillow and blew out the candle. She lay down, clutching Gracie, her fairy doll that Hal had also given her.

She tried to sleep, but sleep was difficult when all you dreamt of were goblins.

* * *

"Do snakes go to heaven?" Gus asked.

He and Eilwen were collaborating on laundry, he rolling the washed clothes, while Eilwen, sopping wet, bent over a tub of soapy water, raked sheets across a scrubboard.

"They go to snake heaven," she answered matter-of-factly.

"Why do you always wanna bury the dead snakes we find, but not the dead anything else we find?"

Eilwen paused. She had never consciously asked herself that before.

"Are snakes your favorite animal?" Gus asked when she didn't respond.

Eilwen nodded. "Yup."

"My favorite animal's an elephant," Gus went on conversationally. "Wanna know why? I learned in school that they're the biggest animal that's not a whale."

He continued prattling away about what he'd learned in school recently, but Eilwen heard only noise. Gus's love for school was one of many differences between the orphaned siblings. Another was Eilwen's frequent need for silence.

Eilwen did not look a thing like her brother. Gus was blond, blue-eyed, and too fair to even freckle – he simply turned red. Meanwhile Eilwen was yellow-eyed and black-haired. And tan. She looked positively brown after toiling in the sun every spring. Though not common, it was widely known that some country families would inexplicably produce swarthy children out of nowhere. It meant the family had "Black Dutch" or "Dark German" somewhere in their history – another taboo of which Eilwen had been lucky enough to receive the full brunt. "Satan had a field day when he made you," Mona had once told her.

Eilwen, still bent over the washtub, lost in thought, suddenly viewed her love of snakes in a negative light.

"You'll make sure they treat my tobacco right, won't you, honey?" Old Hal called from the porch suddenly.

He had been sitting in his rocker since about ten o'clock, watching the children launder in the front yard.

He always seemed to know whenever Eilwen needed uplifting.

Eilwen stood straight. She nodded importantly, bolstered by the magnitude of the task with which Old Hal regularly trusted her. "Yessir, I'll make sure! The dirt already smells great!"

"You always did have a knack for planting." Old Hal's eyes sparkled, the skin around them wrinkling.

In his heyday, Hal T. Hittle had been the guiding hand that had seen his farm become one of the forerunners of tobacco production in this part of Nelson County. He tenaciously claimed the "T" in his name stood for "tobacco," and it very well could have – there was no record it stood for anything else. Despite his booming voice and stubborn, childish tendencies, the man had briefly run a local tobacco empire before complications at the time of the Great War had impacted his trade. It had been difficult for emotional Old Hal to prioritize business when his only son had been across the sea, likely never to return.

But Dale Hittle had returned, and alive at that. And though Hal's trade had never returned to its former grandeur quantity-wise, his tobacco had recently become the most consistently highest graded in the county.

Thanks to Eilwen.

"You knew what good dirt smelled like before you were out of diapers," Hal continued from the porch. "Barely a decade old, and you've already a better flair for air-curing than any farmer I've known in eighty years. I pray it's you who keeps this place running after I'm gone."

"Yeah, but… that won't be for a long time."

Hal chuckled. "Healthier men have died younger, darlin'."

"You're just lucky, then."

Hal started to laugh, but sobered suddenly. "Come 'ere, Eilwen." He beckoned her to the porch. "Gus, go re-hang that sheet. It don't look even."

Gus, who had been about to follow Eilwen to the porch, turned and studied the clothesline. "Which sheet?"

"All of 'em," said Hal. "Just re-hang all of 'em."

Gus groaned and tromped to the clothesline. Eilwen scrambled up the side of the porch.

Hal quickly put out his pipe. His son and daughter-in-law were far more Methodist than he, so he could only smoke when they were away from the farmhouse. But little Eilwen, who had a sensitive nose, was agitated by any form of smoke. She scrunched her nose as she climbed into his lap. The smell of burning tobacco persisted – it clung to his clothes – but she could stomach it for Old Hal. In fact, she had learned to love it for him.

"I am indeed lucky," Hal said. His eyes always smiled before his mouth did. "A man as scatterbrained as I couldn't have run a plantation for so long without luck, eh?"

"You had money."

Hal laughed. "Well, that certainly didn't hinder me. But I had plenty of chances to lose it. Now, darling, I'm going to tell you – and *only* you – the real reason I managed to stay on top as long as I did. The reason I've been so lucky. Probably the reason I haven't died yet. Can you keep a secret?"

Eilwen nodded. After all, she'd kept the pocket watch secret for over a month now, hadn't she?

"Do you want to hear the secret?" Hal asked.

Eilwen nodded, leaning closer.

Hal was practically smirking. "Do you believe in fairies, Eilwen? Answer honestly, now."

Eilwen paused.

What startled her was that she'd wanted to answer *yes*.

"Fairies?" she repeated, as she wasn't sure what else to say. Was this a riddle? Was Hal playing a game with her?

Hal nodded seriously. His demeanor had shifted. "Yes ma'am. Fairies."

"What about them?"

"Exactly what I said. Do you believe in them?"

A small part of Eilwen was inclined to say *no*. As the kids at school would say, she was nine years old, after all. But the part of her that wanted to say *yes* was stronger by far. "I... used to, I suppose. Why's that important?"

"Why is –?" Hal sounded exasperated. "Why, missy, answering this question right is the only way I can know if I should bother telling you anything! Eilwen Tabb, do you believe in fairies, yes or no?"

"I – yes."

"Good girl. Now, why did it take you so long to admit it?"

"Because... well, truthfully, I've never seen a fairy," Eilwen confessed, with the shame of one admitting to having never gone to church. "Besides Gracie," she added, thinking of the doll he'd given her. Hal enjoyed buying the children sweets when the family drove to town on Sundays, but one Sunday a few years back, Hal had bought Eilwen a doll on a whim; he seemed to get pleasure out of making Mona watch him spoil the girl she hated so much. That evening, he'd made Mona sew wings to the back of the doll's dress, turning it into a fairy. Eilwen had never seen daggers sharper than the ones Mona had glared at Hal that night.

"That's exactly right," Hal said. "You're a smart girl. You don't place faith in what you've never seen. People would think you mad. How can you believe in something you haven't seen with your own eyes?"

Eilwen didn't know whether to agree.

"Unless," Hal's voice was low, "someone you know and trust has seen that something for themselves?"

Excitement jolted through her. "You've seen fairies?"

Hal nodded.

Eilwen sat wide-eyed on his lap. Some childish spark within her flared and consumed all trace of developing maturity and reason. Fairies, real! Such a discovery would shed wonder on everything, brighten the world the rest of her days…

…but life with Mona had taught Eilwen that nothing promised ever resembled what she was stirred to imagine. When Eilwen had been promised going to school would be exciting, she'd arrived to be taunted, laughed at, and paddled. When promised a bed of her own, she'd walked upstairs to find a pile of straw in the corner, while Gus snoozed on the cot they'd once shared. What other possibilities were tangled up in that nod Hal had given just now? What *exactly* did the old man mean when he spoke the word "fairy"? When his youthful eyes twinkled in the shade of the oak trees? Eilwen was frightened, though she didn't know why.

"Are you sure?" she asked carefully.

Hal sighed. "Eilwen, if there's one thing I want you to take away from this, it's that you'll never be surer of anything in your life than when you sight your first fairy. Besides, you don't identify one by *looking* at it…" He spoke with the passion of a sermonizing minister, the determination to persuade of a child who has suddenly realized it is possible to argue with adults. "It's a *feeling*. Something you know in your gut. Something you know without thinking. You always *feel* a fairy before you see it. That comes in handy when they're mad at you. Helps you avoid them."

"Mad at you?" Eilwen thought of Gracie's sweet face and couldn't imagine the doll capable of anger toward anyone– even Mona.

"Oh yes, the fairies have nasty little tempers when wronged," Hal said. "They're no more righteous than you or I." He cleared his throat at Eilwen's look of alarm. "But I don't want you fearing them, now. You've always loved them so. They'll be inclined to love you back."

"They are real, then?" Eilwen couldn't help asking.

The old man's eyes held something close to pity. He reached up and stroked a lock of Eilwen's jet-black hair. "I tease you and your brother a lot, Eilwen, but I'm not so cruel as to lead you on about something so dear. What I tell you may not exist the way you've imagined, but that doesn't make it any less real."

Eilwen let her thoughts drift. A breeze picked up, fluttering the oak leaves. She asked, absently, "When did you see your first fairy?"

It was a moment before Hal answered. "Recently. Not long before you were brought to live here. I'd been able to feel them most of my life – sense their presence. But I never saw one until a summer evening six years ago, when I lost my favorite cat to the Fae."

Eilwen gasped.

"Yes. It was a hard loss." Hal nodded pensively, and Eilwen wondered if he was trying not to cry. She patted his hand. "She left me behind. Something in the forest caught her interest that night. She leapt from my lap and ran straight for the trees." Hal waved toward where the woods began behind the curing barn. "And I've not seen her since. Pity, too. She was a unique little thing. Tiny, but vociferous. Had a mind of her own. Unlike any other cat I'd ever known. And she had thumbs."

"*Thumbs?*"

"Aye, sometimes cats are born with thumbs. They're terribly intelligent. Gifted little things. I reckon that gift was what let my Mittens see whatever it was that lured her away that night."

"How did you know it was a fairy she was after?"

"Well, I felt it! That tingling in your stomach that tells you something otherworldly's afoot? I knew what my kitten was after, and I had to follow. Fairies will leave you be if you respect them, but they're unpredictable, and I loved that cat, crazy as she was. I had to know she'd keep safe. I followed her into the woods, sprinting at first, hoping to catch up – but that's a pointless endeavor when chasing a feline, isn't it? So I took to walking, following my gut, and the rustling leaves in her wake. Deeper and deeper into the trees I went. It occurred to me that there shouldn't be so many trees – the woods shouldn't go this far. When suddenly I wasn't in no woods anymore, but a forest, with trees thick as silos, shrouded with sparkling moss and ferns, ancient as the wind.

"I must have rubbed my eyes too much, assessing the conundrum, for I began to see tiny lights around me, of all colors. And just ahead, pouncing after the lights, was my dear Mittens. I was just stepping forward, hoping to reach her, when I saw *him*."

Eilwen's eyes widened. "Who?"

"The devil who lured her away from me." Hal's tone was alarmingly bitter. Eilwen tensed.

"He was a little thing. No bigger than a human tot. But his skin glowed eerily. And his hair... it was redder than the sky at sunset, and just as fiery. He moved toward my darling cat with a grace no mortal possessed. But right before he reached her, he took notice of me, and froze. Mittens froze too.

"That was when I knew I'd lost her – when I saw her respond to that... *being*... better than she'd ever, as smart as she was, responded to me. She followed his gaze, and her eyes finally found me. Not because she'd wanted to find me, nor because she'd sensed me. But because *he* had looked at me. Had he not, I still wonder if I would have gotten that last farewell look into her eyes."

Hal's silence was fitting to his look of pained reminiscence. He soon came back to himself. "He took off into the forest then. She turned and followed. High-tailed after him as though he were made of fish and cream. I never saw her again."

"Why'd he take your cat?"

"Hell if I know, Eilwen. There's no knowing why the Fae do the things they do." Hal started rocking in the chair. He held Eilwen closer. "As I said, they're no more righteous than you or I. But that also means they're no more evil. I like to think there was a reason for what happened that night. But there's just no knowing. Not until I pass on and gain whatever gift it was Mittens had."

"But you can already feel fairies!" Eilwen offered hastily. "That's a gift. You're the only one I've ever met who can do that!"

A chuckle sounded in Hal's throat and he hugged Eilwen, who smiled, enjoying the rare feeling of contentedness she felt right now. How could anyone – even a cat – have ever wanted to leave Old Hal's lap? "It's a gift indeed. The real gift, though, is being able to see them." His pause made Eilwen look at him. "Do you have the Gift?"

"No. I don't know," Eilwen confessed. "How can I find out?"

"That's the secret I'm going to tell you." Hal straightened up. "There are several ways to – *August Henry!*" he roared suddenly, making Eilwen jump. "You re-hang those re-hung sheets! Heavens to Betsy, boy, you're a disgrace to right angles everywhere!"

Gus, who'd been approaching the porch, groaned and turned back toward the clothesline.

Hal shook his head. "What was I saying? Right, how to find… Well, there aren't many ways to test if you have the Gift. Besides seeing a fairy, that is. But there are ways to acquire it. Most do accidentally. Like I did."

"Accidentally?"

"I told you how lucky I was, didn't I?"

Hal reached up under his cap and pulled out a paper-thin something so inconspicuous Eilwen half thought he was holding thin air.

Was he holding a fairy?

Was this a test?

Then she saw it.

"Is that a four-leaf clover?"

Hal smiled at the dry, pressed greenery, twirling it between his thumb and forefinger. "Has to be lucky to've lasted this long."

Eilwen was afraid to breathe. It looked fragile: old, wrinkled, dry enough that exhaling might snap its stem, or knock off that revered fourth leaf. She wondered what kind of secret magic must be holding it together. "This is why you're lucky?"

"And why I can see what others can't."

"How come?"

"Because I found it. All on my own. In the clover patch under the oak where the forest starts." He drifted into a reverie not unlike what Eilwen experienced in the fields. "That's one way to go about it. The easiest. If you're not sure whether you've got the Gift, find a four-leaf clover, and you'll most assuredly gain it."

"So I can see them now?" Eilwen asked enthusiastically.

"No!" Hal snapped, as though it were obvious. "You can't just ride the coattails of someone else's clover! That's not how it works. You need to find one of your own, or there's no magic to it." Hal tucked the clover possessively back up under his cap. "Pretty sure this is why I haven't gone senile yet," he said. "Keeping it near my head all this time."

Eilwen smiled. "When did you *feel* your first fairy, Hal?"

If the question reached Hal, it didn't show for several seconds. "A while back," he said. "A long while."

"How long?"

"When there were still slaves sleeping where you sleep now. I was two years younger than you. Imagine how

22

much fun I could've had if I'd had a four-leaf clover back then." He noticed the spark in Eilwen's yellow eye and figured she must be calculating her own method of locating a four leaf-clover. He would be right. "A word of warning though, dear," he said, his voice suddenly tender. He stroked her cheek, then held her close again, tighter than he'd ever held her before. "Some people, once they've seen the Fae, can never go back to living in this world. And that's why it's so very important, Eilwen, that those who've been touched by magic – as I'm sure you have – are always ready to say some goodbyes."

* * *

Hal died the following week.

Uncle Dale had reportedly searched every pocket of every piece of clothing Hal owned before the burial. His face was quite pale as the casket closed.

Eilwen stood at the gravesite, feeling numb. Not knowing what to feel. She had known all her life she was an orphan, but never before had she felt like one.

Never before had she hated the idea of putting something in the earth so much.

Chapter II

The Flood Orphan

Flow on, thou might river!
High-road of nations, flow!
And thou shalt flow, when all the woods
Upon they sides are low.
Yes, thou shalt flow eternally,
Though on thy peopled shore
The rising town and dawning state
Should sink to rise no more.
– Ephraim Peabody, "The Ohio"

When the commotion over Hal's death had subsided, Mona had taken the grave markers of Dale's relatives in the family plot and used them as stepping stones to create a walkway from the driveway to the porch, and had gone out of her way to make certain that Hal's stone was the last one before the porch steps began, so that no one entering or leaving the house from the front could avoid stepping on it.

Eilwen had been beside herself.

Never before had she wished death on another.

She'd cursed at Mona the day she'd come home from school to see Hal's monument thus defaced. She'd screamed, and thrown things. She'd threatened Mona's life. For a split second, there had been genuine fear in Mona's hardened eyes when Eilwen had bounced back, undaunted, from a smack to the face as though Mona's hand had not even touched her. Likely the only thing that had saved Mona from being bodily harmed by her niece that day had been the sudden roaring wind outside, rattling the shutters and then the rest of the house. Tornado season abruptly reminded them all then that nature ruled no matter what, and Mona, Dale, Gus, and Eilwen had hurried to the cellar to sit in tense and morbid silence until the wind died down.

By then, Eilwen's temper had died. Helpless and trapped underground with the object of her ire, Eilwen had been reduced to sobs. Mostly, at this point in it all, for fear of whatever punishment awaited her.

The apple switch had been bloodied by the time Mona was finished, and such were the lingering wounds that Eilwen had been useless on the farm for two days. In addition to the whipping, Mona had thrown Gracie in the fire.

That night, Eilwen dreamt of a black snake. It had been lost and lonely, forever searching the wilderness for something it couldn't find. When Eilwen awoke she thought of the snake she and Gus had buried down by the creek, with no grave marker to call its own. She'd instinctively reached for Gracie for comfort then remembered what Mona had done, and wept to herself until morning.

She would continue to dream of the lost snake for the next four years. Sometimes days would go between the dreams. Sometimes months. But always the dream returned. Always the golden eyes of the black serpent found her again. And always Eilwen would suddenly feel all was right with the world.

If only for as long as the dream lasted.

By the time Eilwen was thirteen, the Hittle family plot had disappeared, indistinguishable from the rest of the yard. Any passerby would never have guessed that dozens of bodies lay beneath the grass.

Eilwen had memorized exactly where Hal lay, though. She'd counted how many footsteps he was from the house back when the grave had been fresh, knowing Mona would have removed any physical marker she erected.

Eilwen had also managed to save Hal's cap – a remarkable feat, as Mona had determinedly sought out and burned whatever she could find of Hal's. Mona had wanted him eradicated – every trace of his having ever existed wiped from the face of the earth. Eilwen had kept the cap hidden under her bed the summer following his death, but when the first chill of fall arrived that year, a bold streak arrived along with it, and after breakfast Eilwen placed the cap on her head, walked outside (hopping lithely over Hal's stone), and proceeded to wear it proudly around the farm. The first time Mona tried to snatch it from her, Eilwen fearfully but steadfastly fought back. A sudden sharp breeze picked up mid-fight, and Mona, having only just snatched the cap away, threw it on the ground, grinding it into the dust with her shoe. "Fine! Keep it and let your fleas infest it! It's what it deserves!"

It had been Eilwen's first victory since keeping her name.

The cap had been Eilwen's only freedom after losing Hal, and she exploited it. She wore it to school. She wore it in church. She quickly grew immune to the looks and

26

comments of disapproval that followed her everywhere. She'd had practice ignoring them all her life regarding reasons far more disgraceful, and when the looks and comments intensified, her indifference toward them responded in kind.

She simply didn't care anymore.

There came a point when Mona's insults were nothing. Mona's emotional abuse became water off Eilwen's back. There came a point when all Eilwen did was simply avoid the physical punishments when possible, and ignore whatever else Mona and the rest of the world threw at her, growing so distanced from it all that there were even times when the surly behavior of others actually amused her. One day after supper, Eilwen was alone visiting Hal's grave, and suddenly found herself laughing madly.

What more could they take from her?

Why did they even try?

When school started back in the fall of '37, Eilwen was almost happy, for it was the beginning of the end. Her light at the end of the tunnel. Her last year in institutionalized education. Gus would continue to attend High School when his time came, being the male heir: the basket into which Mona and Dale had been devotedly putting their eggs since the childless couple had taken him and his bastard sister into their care. But Eilwen's post-eighth grade education was up in the air; and as much as Mona loved going out of her way to make Eilwen suffer, Eilwen doubted Mona would force her to attend school any longer. The Hittles were already shorthanded for a farming family.

Then Eilwen could be free. She could spend her days – year-round – planting and being outside. There was nowhere to go but up.

But first she had to get through this year.

"I'd better not hear one word from Miss Ethel about you," Mona threatened casually on the first morning of school, just as the depressing building appeared round a turn. She had spent most of the drive complaining about the inevitable misdemeanors of her own students before finally getting around to Eilwen's hypothetical sins. It took her longer than usual at least, thought Eilwen, who, squeezed uncomfortably between Mona and Gus in the Ford pickup, recited dryly, "Yes, ma'am."

"I've a nice pliant switch picked out for you, 'cause I know from heartbreaking experience my words'll do you no good."

Eilwen nodded, trying not to roll her eyes.

Mona yanked Eilwen's hair. "You hear me? You say *Yes, ma'am* when I speak to you! God, you've given me the most abhorrent reputation! I can barely show my face at meetings or picnics because of you and your sass!"

"Yes, ma'am."

"…and the looks I get!" Mona was still ranting, her start-of-a-new-school-year tantrum being by far one of her most martyrly of the year, surpassed only by her my-cobbler-should've-won-first-prize tantrum that followed the school picnic every spring. "All for fostering my whoring sister's bastard! Only Christ knows my suffering. Only Christ, also tortured for doing good, knows this agony. I haven't been invited to a proper luncheon in months!"

They pulled into the parking lot and unbuckled. (Except for Eilwen, who had no seatbelt; she kept waiting for the day Mona would decide to stop the truck short and send her flying through the windshield.) Eilwen and Gus grabbed their books from the backseat, being two of the handful of students who begin the first day already equipped thanks to their guardian being a teacher, then followed Mona to the school building. When they reached it Mona stopped and faced them.

"There's a new boy starting today. I don't know much about him, since because of Eilwen no one talks to me. All I know is his name's McAtee and he's Thelma Duvall's nephew. Which means he's a Catholic, so neither of you are to speak to him."

"Miss Thelma has a nephew?" Gus asked. "How come we ain't seen him before?"

Eilwen could understand his confusion. Thelma Duvall lived just one farm over from the Hittles.

"He's from Louisville," Mona said, opening the door and ushering her niece and nephew inside.

"How come he's going to school so far away from Louisville?"

"Because he moved here to live with Thelma."

"Why'd he move here?"

"Oh, I don't know, his parents died or something. Hold still, August." Mona bent and tidied his blond hair with her hand, then licked her thumb and rubbed a smudge of dirt off his cheek. She gave him a strange look. "You're starting to freckle."

"Can I wear a hat like Uncle when I work the fields?" Gus asked excitedly.

29

"No!" Mona snapped. "Get to class, both of you. Eilwen, remember: *not one word.*"

Eilwen nodded boredly, then hastily added, "Yes, ma'am."

Mona glared after her until she disappeared down the hall.

Eilwen hated this hall. She hated this building. Chipping paint, cinderblock walls, bars of unnatural light... The very skeleton felt evil. The classroom was not so bad, being naturally sunlit, but the one thing Eilwen detested above all else – more than the artificial lighting – were the wood-iron folding-seat desks.

It was an irrational hatred. She couldn't give a reason for it. Maybe it was the uncomfortable way the benches were carved, or the forced connection to another student's workspace. But whatever the reason, Eilwen was always the last to sit in the mornings and the first out of her seat when the bell rang in the afternoons; she could never seem to get away from her desk fast enough. Sitting in it stimulated the same exhausted impatience she always seemed to suffer after plowing every spring. But at least when plowing, she was outside.

She lingered by the window, gazing at the woods behind the playground.

Miss Ethel entered the room some minutes later.

"Good morning, Eilwen," she said coldly.

Eilwen returned the greeting, feigning obliviousness to her coldness.

Miss Ethel did not detest Eilwen for being a brown-skinned bastard so much as she did for the fact that Eilwen had once begun an argument with her – and shamelessly prolonged it – in front of the whole class. And ultimately both defeated Ethel's platform and blasphemed at the same time. Eilwen had simply wondered aloud whether or not the serpent in the Garden of Eden was actually evil, or if the people who'd written the Bible had tried to make it *appear* evil. Though as innocent as Eilwen believed the inquiry, the exchange had grown heated, and Eilwen had run into the woods after school and walked home that day to avoid the truck ride with Mona. The next morning, however, Mona had dragged her by the ear into Ethel's room, and made her stand at the front and read aloud from a piece of paper stating that she was "a hopeless, wicked, evil child who with her heathen ways and pagan obsessions is paving her way straight to Hell," among other things Mona had written. Mona had had her own class to teach and so hadn't stayed to watch Eilwen, who had thus recited the paper in a bored drawl, clearly mocking the situation and all involved; she'd managed to get some giggles out of her astounded classmates before Ethel had taken the cane to her hands.

The rest of the students arrived. Eilwen was forced to sit. Agnes Steckler, the closest thing she had to a friend, sat behind her.

Every fall, Agnes' family paid Eilwen a quarter for her help harvesting their own meager tobacco crop, even though the Stecklers knew any money they gave Eilwen ended up Mona's; it was unspokenly acknowledged that they were paying Mona to let Eilwen be free of her for a few hours a day.

"I had the dream again last night," Eilwen whispered to Agnes.

"About the snake?" Agnes asked concernedly.

"I think it's a sign." Eilwen shifted uncomfortably in her seat. "It was closer than it's ever been before. I never saw it this clear. You think it means something's gonna happen?"

Agnes shook her head. "You've been having that dream for years," she said, kindly enough that Eilwen knew she was not simply being dismissive. "If something was gonna happen, it'd have happened by now."

Eilwen was silent.

"This'll be our last harvest together," Agnes whispered semi-sadly, while Miss Ethel began the roll. "Mama's letting me live with my sister next year so I can go to Louisville Girls' High!"

Eilwen smiled and congratulated her, hoping her enthusiasm did not sound forced.

"McAtee?"

Miss Ethel was louder than normal, suggesting she'd already called the name. "Dristan McAtee?" Her eyes scanned every seat. She shook her head. "Not a grand start."

"Ooooh, the new boy!" Agnes squeaked. She tapped Eilwen's shoulder, and Eilwen automatically flinched in response. "Your aunt's a teacher – has she heard anything about him? I haven't heard much, other than he's from Louisville. One of those lace-curtain Irish near the river..."

Agnes spoke with familiarity on the subject while Eilwen simply nodded. This was their formula: Agnes, whose widespread socialite family was in the know, relayed information, and Eilwen, who was always last to know, prayed her ignorance went unnoticed, or at least un-commented upon. *Lace-curtain Irish…* The most Eilwen knew about anything Irish was that her aunt's and mother's grandparents had haled from Ireland, and that Hal's mother had survived the potato famine by immigrating to America. But how any of that could be connected to window treatments, she hadn't the faintest.

When attendance was over, the class was led in morning prayer (the few Catholic children making their presence awkwardly known by crossing themselves), and lessons began.

At lunch, all the girls Eilwen's age spoke of was the absent new boy, who had either stupidly or devilishly missed the first day of school. They sat in a circle beneath a tree at the end of the schoolyard, Eilwen having obtained an invitation from being in Agnes' vicinity. Three feet away, the forest began. A brook babbled a little ways in. After five minutes of listening to nothing but talk of the new boy, Eilwen decided the water was more interesting and gave its sound her full attention.

"Mama told me he's one of those flood victims we've been hearing of," a girl named Joyce was saying. "You know, from the winter flood?"

"You mean *you've* been hearing of," said Agnes jealously. "You're the only one of us with a radio."

"I'm only saying I bet that's why he's not here. Maybe he's homesick. Misses his parents. And his old school."

"City folks *are* as wimpy as Pa says," said a girl named Martha. "Don't he have brothers or sisters? When my momma died, me and my sisters kept each other, Pa, *and* the farm going."

"Nope, just his aunt. City folks don't like having kids too much. My cousin in Cincinnati just had her second baby and already acts like she won't have anymore."

"But he's Irish, ain't he? They can't not have kids. They'll go to Hell."

"Maybe he was adopted. Like Eilwen." Agnes' face brightened. "Say, that'll give us a way to introduce ourselves! He'll love to know if he already has something in common with one of us!"

Eilwen, snapped out of daydreaming at hearing her name, realized Agnes, Joyce and Martha were staring at her. "What?" she asked dumbly, still half-focused on the sound of the brook.

"Oh, would you?" Agnes took Eilwen's arm. Jumpy from years of Mona's beatings, Eilwen flinched away at the unexpected touch, but Agnes continued, "It'd make it so much easier for everyone! Especially since he's already missed the first day."

Eilwen opened and closed her mouth. "I still don't know what you –"

"You'll be the first one to make friends with the McAtee boy," Martha summarized decidedly – the first time she had directly addressed Eilwen since the sixth grade. "You're both orphans. It only makes sense."

"And then you can introduce him to us," said Joyce, betraying their underlying goal.

Eilwen mentally sighed. The last thing she wanted to do was help these girls chase a boy. It was tobacco season: she had better and more important things to focus on.

"Please, Eilwen?" Agnes begged.

"Why can't one of you talk to him?" Eilwen demanded.

"Oh, Eilwen, don't be such a ninny! Do this one thing for us?"

Eilwen was about to relent and agree when she remembered something that saved her: "I can't anyway. He's Catholic. Aunt won't let me talk to him."

"…Oh." Agnes looked at the grass, defeated.

Martha crossed her arms. "She's so judgmental."

"Maybe we can accidentally knock into him on our way to lunch tomorrow," Joyce suggested.

"Or trip him in the hall, and introduce ourselves when we apologize…"

Talk spiraled into ways in which the girls could "accidentally" strike up a conversation with the new boy. Eilwen leaned back in the grass and pulled Hal's cap down over her face.

School couldn't have ended early enough. Eilwen sat perched on the hitching post where the students who lived near the school tethered the ponies they rode, watching Agnes try to calm Honeysuckle, her small mare. "Today wasn't so bad, was it? For a first one?" Agnes said as she mounted. "Calm down, Honeysuckle. Gosh, something's got her spooked. Anyway, and tomorrow we'll meet the new boy! If he shows up.

"Try not to think too much on things," she said with a seriousness that caught Eilwen off guard. "You dream about fairies all the time and have yet to meet any. I think you're safe from the snake."

Eilwen, oddly discomforted, waved goodbye as Agnes left.

She heard Mona's footsteps inside the school and made a dash for the truck, where Gus squatted amongst a group of boys who were prodding something in the dirt with a stick. "What've you got there?" she asked, peering over his blond head.

"A snake!" one of Gus's friends piped. "It slithered under your all's truck, and Gus is coaxing it out!"

"With a stick?"

"A *coaxing* stick," the boy corrected.

Eilwen got down on hands and knees to look under the truck.

Before she even saw the snake, she felt a tremor in her stomach – a flipping sensation like flying – that only intensified when she laid eyes on it. There, coiled directly beneath where Eilwen had sat on the drive over, was a snake black as night.

It was beautiful. Motionless. The way its loosely coiled body was layered suggested it was of decent length. Eilwen swallowed a gasp, for the serpent was staring her down with yellow eyes – eyes that, despite her better judgment, she thought looked gawking and curious. An impulse of which she had no conscious awareness had her reaching toward it…

"Eilwen." Gus shook her shoulder. "Aunt's coming."

Eilwen jerked, scrambling to her feet, dust wafting around her. The boys jumped back, shouting and babbling.

"Did it strike?"

"Here, take the stick for protection!"

"We're leaving now." Mona strode through the boys clustered around her truck without hesitation. None was needed: they parted obediently.

"Miss Mona? Ma'am? There's a snake under your truck, ma'am," one boy warned.

"Did you hear it rattle?" Mona asked tersely.

The boys shook their heads.

"What shape was its head?"

"I reckon regular-shaped, ma'am."

"Then it's harmless," Mona declared, jerking open the driver's side door. "Pity. I'd rather run over a copperhead than one of the good'uns."

"*What?* No! Don't run over it!"

Eilwen knew the instant the words left her mouth she'd be in trouble.

The driver's side door slammed shut.

Mona walked around the front of the truck to stand before Eilwen, who was determined not to flinch, despite the cold sweat she'd broken into. It was one thing to openly challenge Mona in the privacy of the Homestead, where even that was guaranteed a smack to the face or days without supper.

It was quite another to do so in public.

The silence that followed stretched on forever. "So close," Mona hissed at last. "So close to being a good day for you. Miss Ethel said you were tolerable today, but if *this* is what she calls 'tolerable,' I wonder at her competence."

Eilwen stood tensely, eyes locked on Mona's chin. All she could think right now was that she hoped the snake slithered away in time.

Mona stalked back to the driver's side. "I'll have to whip you every night, regardless of Ethel's reports. Clearly she can't be trusted." She looked at Eilwen again before getting in the truck. "And why are you covered in dirt? You're walking home!"

Mona started the engine. Gus looked hesitant to comply to her order that he get in the truck, but eventually obeyed, mouthing *I'm sorry* to his big sister as he shut the door.

Eilwen watched the truck roll away, then looked down at her clothes, wondering about the dirt Mona had mentioned. She must have dirtied her clothes while kneeling down to see –

She fell back to the ground, searching for the snake, though she didn't know why: such a black creature should have easily stood out on the dirt and gravel. But it was nowhere to be seen.

But there was no blood, either. No sign tires had touched the fragile mail of reptile skin. Even so, distress must have shown on Eilwen's face, for a voice beside her said, "I saw it slither into the woods."

She turned to see the boy who'd offered her the stick: Thomas Ruckriegal, youngest of the Ruckriegal brood. As the oldest was nearing thirty and a decade had passed since Thomas's birth, it was likely he'd remain the youngest.

Eilwen swallowed. "It's okay?"

"Mmhm. It got away. I'm sorry, Miss Eilwen. My mom and pop don't like the way your aunt treats you. It ain't your fault you're a darkie bastard, after all."

Eilwen smiled at the boy as authentically as she could. "It's just a mile or three, Thomas, I don't have far to walk."

"I don't mean the walking. If a little walking gets you, you got no business on a farm, and you seem to run yours pretty good." Thomas tipped his cap and started down the road.

Eilwen remained where she was for some time, staring longingly across the yard separating the school and woods. She could still hear the creek, invisible but babbling, tumbling over log and rock, with pockets of silence where it pooled and deepened. There was a comfort to the thought that the snake's haven was so near. For reasons she couldn't explain, knowing it was just beyond the forest edge made the thought of school more bearable.

As Eilwen slowly walked the road alone, she wondered how Agnes would have reacted if she'd stuck around long enough to see the snake. She wouldn't still think the dreams didn't mean anything, would she?

What would Hal have thought of the dreams?

Dreams were Hal's playground. He'd thrived in them. That night he'd spoken of four years ago – the night he claimed to have lost his kitten to the fairies – could have been a dream, visiting him after his loss to ease his pain. Was that, perhaps, what the snake in Eilwen's dreams (and under the truck) was trying to do? Comfort her?

…Was Hal the snake?

Eilwen shook her head. No, there was more to the snake than Hal trying to comfort her. And if he were, he'd do it in ways that didn't result in her being guaranteed a whipping every night as far out as she could see. Besides, Hal had never talked about snakes.

Perhaps her dreams were omens. But Eilwen always felt comforted and happy when the snake visited her, so omen couldn't be right either. The snake felt important. The more Eilwen thought about the snake, the dearer it became. Perhaps it was a sign, yes, but certainly no omen.

The black ones couldn't hurt you. If one bit you, your hand didn't swell.

It was an August afternoon, but crisp and bright. The woods around the school spread a ways down Cooney Road, so Eilwen had trees, tall and silent, shading her on either side. There was a rejuvenating wetness to the air; she could smell the atmosphere changing. Fall was the most magical time of year.

For Eilwen, though, the central joy of it all was the tobacco harvest: a relieving, stimulating break from the mindless care of corn and wheat. Tobacco care was an art; the tobacco her masterpiece; the harvest the bittersweet end to the creative process that stretched through spring and summer. It brought a sense of accomplishment, which was something Eilwen found nowhere else. Though the name *Hittle* was on it when it was packed and sold, it was *her* tobacco. *She* was the one who, knee-deep in mud, hand-shoveled excess water from the roots when it over rained. *She* was the one who double-checked Gus's sloppy topping job every week. *She* was the one sent scrambling to the highest beams of the curing barn, risking her life to ensure the leaves were spaced *just right.*

Most importantly, *she* was the one Old Hal had trusted to take care of it when he was gone. That tobacco was hers. That moody, sensitive plant that withers at the slightest alteration in sun or soil was a crop the faint of heart could not endeavor to raise, and Eilwen Tabb took exceptional pride in that.

She was kicking an acorn along the road when a movement to her left caught her eye.

She halted, peering into the roadside ditch crammed with the green remains of now bloom-less lilies. Something had rustled in them. Normally Eilwen would assume a bird or chipmunk, but something felt too coincidental, too important…

She continued walking, but the rustling recurred. She stopped, locking eyes on the ditch, then got down on hands and knees and peered into the shadowy forest of lily leaves. No movement anymore. The feeling of importance that had flared a moment ago dimmed, but it hadn't died.

If she'd been less focused on the rustling leaves, Eilwen would have noticed the approach of a stranger on the road – heard alien footsteps grow nearer, louder. As it was, the prospect of potentially spying the black snake from the schoolyard among the dying ditch lilies had so enraptured her that most of the world – indeed, what many would call the *real* world – was blocked out. And so it startled her greatly when a polite voice that was nonetheless too near for comfort inquired, "Have you lost something, miss?"

Eilwen gasped and stood with panicked swiftness, eyes falling on a young man to her right.

"Oh, I'm sorry. Didn't mean to startle you," he said.

Eilwen blinked. The boy did not look familiar. He didn't even sound familiar, for he spoke with a clipped and sophisticated twang that Eilwen had only heard the few times she'd traveled north – the sort of speech that shamefully reminded her how very much the country drawl of Bardstown shaped her words. That, along with the boy's disarmingly blue eyes, kept her quiet.

"You all right? Here." The boy bent down and collected Eilwen's books, which she'd tossed to the ground in her frenzy to search the lilies. "If you've lost something, I'll help you find it. What were you searching for in the ditch there?"

Eilwen never realized how idiotic her endeavors were until they were questioned. Daydreaming about fairies was never stupid until Agnes asked what she was thinking about. Hunting for four-leaf clovers never seemed pointless until Gus asked what she was looking for. Trying to find a magical snake she'd been convinced was following her hadn't seemed dumb at all until a moment ago.

"Nothing," she stammered, taking her books. "Just, uh... you know... smelling the flowers."

The boy looked amused. "There aren't any flowers."

Eilwen pretended to nod as though just realizing this, then held out her hand. "Well, nice to meet you."

The boy smiled and shook it. He could not have been more than a year or two older than she, judging from the narrowness of his shoulders and the rest of his comparatively tall body, but he carried himself with a maturity that, no matter his age, seemed well beyond his years. His chestnut hair was thick and wavy – almost curly. His eyes were bluer than the sky. "I'm sorry to bother you. I've clearly interrupted a thought," he said laughingly. "But I don't think we've met yet. Dristan McAtee." He bowed slightly.

Eilwen only stared. "Aren't you the new boy everyone's talking about?"

Dristan shrugged, still smiling. "I wouldn't know who's talking about me. Hope they're saying nice things."

"They say you're an orphan."

Dristan's smile turned stiff. "They would be right."

Eilwen pressed her lips, realizing her faux-pas. And feeling guilty for knowing she was about to intentionally commit another. "You'll forgive me, Mr. McAtee –"

"Dristan."

"But I really need to be going. Right away." She waved goodbye to soften her sudden exit, then resumed walking down the road, this time speedily.

She mentally panicked when Dristan caught up and asked if he'd offended her.

"No, I'm just not allowed to talk to you," she tried to explain. "And I'm already in trouble."

Dristan looked puzzled. "Not allowed to talk to me?"

"You're Catholic, aren't you?"

Understanding dawned on Dristan's face. "Well, I live on Lily Lane, and we're almost there," he said instead of answering the question. "Can I just walk with you until then?"

"No, 'cause you can see Lily Lane from my house, and my aunt might see me with you." Eilwen hated how sharp she sounded. "I'm sorry, I don't mean to come off so heartless, 'specially with you being orphaned now and all. I wish I could be nicer to you. I really do."

"What's keeping you from it?" Dristan sounded more curious than hurt.

"My aunt."

"You're Eileen, aren't you?"

"Eil*wen*," she corrected, emphasizing the double-u.

"Oh, beg pardon. My aunt's mentioned you and your brother. You all are orphans too?"

Eilwen nodded, thinking of Hal. She remembered suddenly the sinking feeling she'd felt at his funeral. The jarring emptiness of standing by his fresh grave. The terrible gravity of first realizing she would never hear his voice again.

Dristan had just experienced all that times two.

Eilwen began walking slowly. "How are you holding up?"

Dristan shrugged. "Still in shock. That's what Aunt Thelma says, anyway. I think she's in shock too. She lost a sister."

"At least you have each other."

"Yeah. This all has made me appreciate everything more. I had it pretty good. I'm still lucky, the way I see it. I'm not wading through muck trying to find the floor to my house, at least."

"Was your house spared?"

"Oh no, not even the floor's there anymore. We were right on the river. Near Portland."

Eilwen merely nodded, possessing no knowledge of River City intricacies.

"It was our own fault," Dristan continued, unprompted. "The flood. All our faults. Yes, the rain was bad, but we never gave the river the room it needed. All rivers need wiggle room – you never know what they're gonna do. People keep talking about how the Ohio invaded our homes, but really, we invaded it. Both banks are packed with neighborhoods, and factories... You can't do that to a river. They don't like to feel trapped."

The rest of the walk, though brief, was surprisingly pleasant considering the topic of conversation. Dristan rambled unhappily about his lost home and family, but his mood shifted when he began volunteering brighter details about the flood. His eyes sparkled when he told Eilwen of how he and his friends had once sneaked into Churchill Downs to watch from the stands as some older boys raced each other on rafts around the flooded racetrack. He laughed openly while recounting a story he'd heard about giant catfish swimming through the lobby of The Brown Hotel. He sounded awed when he told of how the water had risen to the point where a be-pedestaled statue of Abraham Lincoln outside the city library had appeared to be walking on water.

Eilwen let him talk. He sounded as though he needed it. Here was this social city boy used to constant crowds and noise, who, on top of having lost his parents, had been suddenly thrust into the quiet stillness of the country with only his mother's sister for companionship. Eilwen would be surprised if he wasn't in shock.

"...and, well, listen to me. I'm sorry to have unloaded on you so much." Dristan rubbed the back of his neck, appearing shy or nervous for the first time. They had reached Lily Lane. "Thanks for the pleasure of walking home with you. I'm sure I'll see you at school tomorrow... Eilwen, was it?"

"Strange names run in my family," Eilwen defended. "I'm told my mother's was so unpronounceable they skipped her eulogy."

"How'd she die?" There was a pitiful combination of empathy and relief in his expression.

"In childbirth. My brother's. My father was a fiendish drunk with no sense of responsibility." Eilwen mindlessly repeated the words Mona had instilled in her all her life.

"I'm sorry. I suppose you carry something of your mother on, though, with that name of yours." Dristan placed his hands in his pockets and looked down Cooney Road. "You say you can see my street from your house?"

Eilwen nodded toward the distant poplar cabin obscured by the oaks in its front yard.

"We'll have to have you over for lunch one day," he said. "My aunt's been itching to show me off to everyone. She keeps hinting at wanting other kids over. I know she's just trying to make me feel as welcome as possible. Makes me feel even guiltier for skipping school today...

"I felt I had to, though," Dristan went on, speaking as though he were trying to explain rather than justify something to himself. "It was the strangest thing, Eilwen – did I say that right? I just... couldn't find it in me to take those final steps. Everything else in my life's taken such a final turn, school was the only thing that hadn't yet. Part of me felt that as long as I hadn't started school here, my life in Louisville was still intact. As long as I hadn't started school, it was easy to pretend I was just spending the last bit of summer with my aunt. That my real school was still waiting for me, by the river.

"And besides, something in the woods kept rustling."

Eilwen looked at him, more interested in his words than ever.

"Spent a good bit of the morning looking for it, though I expect I was looking for any excuse to be late. I could have imagined the rustling. But by the time I realized I was an hour late for school, I figured I may as well skip the whole day. Never did find it, whatever was following me. To be honest, Eilwen, I'd hoped you'd seen it too, when you were searching the ditch back there. At least then I'd know I wasn't imagining things."

Chapter III

Fainting Spells

Yes, we must love! for there is placed
In every living breast a waste –
A desert, where the cheerful green
Of blest Oasis is not seen: –
A void that never can be filled
Until the soul be waked and thrill'd
By that electric flash that starts
The callous Self-God from our hearts
– Jouett Vernon Cosby, "Consecration: A Poem"

Eilwen's shoulder cried out as she lay back. Mona had drawn blood with the switch, and though the bleeding had stopped, the sting remained.

Too much had happened today; there was too much to think on. And Eilwen spent too much time in her head as it was. She wished she would pass out, not to escape the pain, but to escape the swirling fogginess of her mind.

Which was why the curing barn had called to her. She lay up on one of the highest rafters, where her tobacco would soon hang in a few weeks' time, gazing at the roof. Utter silence soothed her there. No noise but the occasional soft flutter of a barn swallow hopping from beam to beam. The air was still but magical in this quiet wooden barn. Eilwen often thought that if she spent enough time in here – if she hung from her rafter long enough – the air would transform her as it did the tobacco. Change her into a better version of herself: an Eilwen people wanted. An Eilwen people would, in the long run, realize was worth the trouble.

But how could Eilwen be worth anything – even the attention of a boy as nice as Dristan – when she felt incapable of worth? Of loving anything? All her love had died with Hal. The only thing she loved now was a plant that couldn't love her back no matter how much she cared for it.

She felt suddenly dizzy, which was odd. She never felt dizzy in the curing barn. Heights had never bothered her.

Dristan seemed so nice and normal; Eilwen was terrified of him ever discovering how twisted her own sense of normalcy was. It was better to never speak with him again anyway – to let him go on with his shallow but at least positive first impression of her – than to allow him to become too familiar with her and thus repulsed in some way. But then… was not his own sense of normalcy twisted now as well? Hadn't his own life been thrown into chaos? Maybe Eilwen and Dristan had more in common than she had allowed herself to consider before meeting him. Yes, he was a city boy and a Catholic, but those first two strikes aside, Eilwen had found his company alarmingly compatible. Agnes Steckler had never even inspired such a feeling in Eilwen.

Maybe Agnes had been right: maybe Dristan needed to know he had something in common with someone. Maybe that was what Eilwen needed as well, and maybe Eilwen and Dristan *would* be friends. The girls at school could have Dristan as a boyfriend for all Eilwen cared. She simply wanted a friend.

Why – oh why – did he have to be Catholic?

Eilwen rubbed her eyes. Her vision was splotchy. She scrambled down from the rafters before she got so dizzy she fell.

Gus wandered into the barn through the main doorway just as Eilwen reached the ground. He asked, almost exhaustedly, "Why did you even say anything earlier? You *know* what Aunt's temper is."

"I couldn't let her run over the snake."

Gus began nodding before Eilwen had even finished the sentence. "It okay?"

"Yeah, it got away."

"You okay?"

Eilwen shrugged.

Gus hugged her. Eilwen gasped, but after a few seconds hugged him back. "Dinner's ready," Gus said. "Aunt said for you to get firewood, then come eat."

Gus left, and Eilwen laced her boots up over her pants then exited the curing barn through the side facing away from the house. She made for the hill with the oak tree behind which the woods began. The wind picked up.

The sun was set, but there was enough light to see. Eilwen gathered what she could carry of the fallen limbs scattered in the grass around the oak. The wind picked up again, stronger than before, and Eilwen set the branches down for a moment to stand with her head held back, relaxing in the wind that gathered unhindered at the top of the hill. The air howled. The oak leaves cheered madly but voicelessly as their tree bent and swayed. The trees in the woods wavered and creaked, the flora on the woods' edge bobbing and flailing; the thousands of tiny leaves whipping up and down looked like a thousand blinking eyes.

With all the commotion, it seemed impossible that one rustle from a wild blackberry bush should catch Eilwen's eye, and yet it had. It was the same reaction she'd had while walking home earlier, when the roadside lilies rustled. She simply *knew* something was there.

Tensing, Eilwen focused on the dark spot between two bobbing canes. She stepped toward the woods, captivated by what looked like a pair of actual eyes. But they vanished with the next gust, disappearing into flickering leaves.

Eilwen felt a shiver that had nothing to do with the wind.

She blinked to clear her vision, trying to clear her head. The eyes had been burnt orange, amid blackberry leaves of the same color. Surely she was imagining things. Yet she kept staring.

She ended her hilltop visit as she always did: with a brief examination of the clover patch beneath the oak. As had been the case every day for the past four years, she found nothing, but something in the air that evening made her feel closer than usual.

As she descended the hill, arms piled with oak branches, she did not notice the black snake that slithered after her. It stopped right as Eilwen passed the curing barn, not yet daring to venture further, but lifted its head above the grass, as a sea serpent would the water, and flicked its tongue, tasting the air through which Eilwen had walked.

* * *

Gus had offered Eilwen his cot that night so that her straw bed wouldn't scratch her back. Eilwen dreamt of the snake again, and when she woke the next morning, she was smiling to herself. Perhaps because Gus's bed had let her sleep so well. But despite how well-rested she should have been, Eilwen found herself more foggy-minded than ever that day. Everything felt fuzzy. Every little noise irritated. Eilwen had always been sensitive to sound and smell, but today her senses overwhelmed her. Far more than she was used to. Half-awake and half-aware, she'd accidentally told Mona to "shut up" during breakfast when Mona had been ranting to Uncle about how awful her students were.

At least the smack to the face had woken Eilwen up a little more.

School was more painful than usual, and for no identifiable reason at all. Eilwen felt sick to her stomach just walking into the building. The thought of her desk physically repulsed her today. She stood at the window, taking in the natural outside world for as long as she could before Ethel finally fussed at her to sit down. Eilwen immediately felt sicker when she did. Her head throbbed.

She hadn't even noticed Dristan that morning. She didn't notice him at all until Agnes, Joyce, Martha, and several other girls clustered around him during lunch. Eilwen wondered if he'd tried to say hi to her and she'd been too fuzzy-headed to notice. She hoped he didn't think she was snubbing him.

Whether he thought that or not, though, Dristan seemed happy. The girls had invited him to eat with them under their tree, and he was smiling an easy-going smile, delighted and comfortable with the attention. Eilwen felt an unpleasant turning in her stomach. She cut open her apple with her pocketknife and resigned herself to eating alone in the shade some distance away. Instead of re-pocketing the knife, she found herself wanting to leave it on the ground. Several inches away from her. It was the oddest impulse, but she couldn't fight it.

She had just started on the second half of her apple when she heard Dristan's voice, intense and curious, stand out from the giggling: "Is there a creek in these woods?"

He had not asked conversationally; it was not a question to move talk along or fill silences. Eilwen turned to watch, curious.

"Yes, there's a crick," Agnes answered, clearly confused at his urgency. "It's a little ways in, though."

"Would you like to see it? I'll take you!" Joyce began packing away her half-eaten lunch.

"Oh no, that's fine." Dristan raised his hands to stop her. "I'll go on my own." He stood and, without any hesitation, a farewell, or even a polite tip of his cap, stepped over Joyce's lunch and strode into the trees and disappeared. Eilwen could hear his feet crunching on the leafy earth long after she could no longer see him, though the other girls didn't seem to notice: they resumed talking as if there were no noise, speculating confusedly over what could have possessed the new boy to act in such a way.

"Must be a flood thing," Martha declared. "Some sick obsession with water. I knew he couldn't be so handsome without a catch."

"Think he's ill?" asked Joyce.

"All city folks are. People ain't meant to live crammed together like that."

"I'm sure he's feeling sentimental is all," Agnes defended. "He did grow up near a river."

"No excuse for lack of manners. We're ladies. He didn't even excuse himself."

Eilwen wondered what had possessed him as well. He had mentioned yesterday – both to Eilwen's bewilderment and relief – that he, too, had felt something following him along the roadside. He, too, had felt a curious inclination to investigate, to the point where he'd sacrificed his entire first day of school, risking who knows what kind of punishment from his aunt for doing so. Had he felt that inclination again? Felt he was being followed again? Perhaps he, too, had seen what had appeared to be eyes watching him from the trees, and the creek was his excuse to investigate.

She wondered if she should go help him. If he did find what had been following them yesterday afternoon, Eilwen wanted to be there for it. But then... she wasn't currently feeling the same draw to the woods that she had felt toward the ditch lilies yesterday. Yesterday, she'd *known* something was in the leaves. It had been a gut feeling she couldn't ignore.

She had no such feeling toward the creek or the woods today.

She sighed down at her apple, feeling suddenly empty. Alone. She'd wanted to feel that pull again: that unignorable mental insistence that something special was happening to her. All she'd felt today, though, was dizzy. If she was feeling a pull at all, her mind was too groggy –

too inundated with unusually intense daily stimuli – to recognize it. She wondered if she was growing ill.

Suddenly an earsplitting shriek ripped the air.

Eilwen bolted upright, head and ears ringing.

She looked around wildly. As the noise tapered off, it became recognizable as a horse's cry.

None of the students' ponies were visible from where Eilwen sat, but she could hear their stamping hooves cut the ground as clearly as if she herself were the ground they struck. Vibrations bombarded her through the air and the earth. Her vision blurred.

However, no one else in the schoolyard seemed concerned. None of the other students jumped at the barrage of sound, or did more than lift their heads in curiosity. They went on talking to each other, playing guessing games or hide-and-seek, or chasing each other with sticks they pretended were bayonets. None of them seemed affected. None of them appeared dizzied or disoriented. Was Eilwen the only one experiencing the clamor? Were the other children deaf? Had they skin of stone?

Rubbing her head, which was still ringing, Eilwen carefully stood and made her way to the front of the school. Though their shrieks had subsided, the ponies continued to jerk and snort and trot in place. Honeysuckle in particular was agitated; Eilwen had never seen the pony's eyes so wide.

"What's wrong, girlie?" Eilwen took the pony's head and held it, trying to calm her. Honeysuckle complied, but only for a moment: the ponies around her were still unsettled and she took up her nervous behavior again, snorting and bobbing.

Eilwen's own head began to throb. The ringing worsened. Her vision blurred again. She rubbed her ears, which were suddenly sore, and held them as she watched the ponies. "What on earth, you all?" she said angrily. The noise was making her head split. "You're acting like you've seen a –"

Eilwen, through her fuzzy vision, looked around for the snake. Every movement she made – even moving her eyeballs – felt electric and heavy. Slow and deliberate, requiring too much focus and effort. It drained her. She felt like an infant learning to control her motor skills all over again. Learning what it felt like to lift an arm, or bend a knee, and learning what it felt like to will those movements to happen.

Or maybe she wasn't learning. Maybe she was losing.

Her blurred vision began to fade altogether. Spots appeared. She stumbled. The earth continued bombarding her with the vibrations of everything that hit it. The air pelted her with vibrations of everything that moved. Eilwen's senses exploded.

What was wrong with her? Had she contracted some disease? Had she been bitten by something? She hadn't a clue, and could not waste time figuring it out. She was losing herself, and still didn't know if the snake was near or not. She had to know. This was too important, too much of a coincidence, too much of everything...

Eilwen stumbled over to Mona's truck. Had her head not been pounding, she would have noticed how her stomach flipped – how her heart leapt into her mouth.

She had shut her eyes as she got down to look beneath the truck, but when she opened them the first thing she thought was that she never wanted to close them again.

The black snake was there, its bright eyes so fixated on Eilwen that anyone else would have fidgeted under such an intimate stare. Anyone else would have looked away, not for fear of being stared down by a snake, but for the feeling of having your very soul pierced. The creature lifted its head shakily, showing no aggression, no fear. And yet Eilwen quickly realized she was sweating.

"Huah!" she gasped, stumbling to her feet. Her hands were soaked in perspiration. She swallowed and rolled her shoulders; the rest of her body was sweating, too.

She stared at her glistening hands. What was wrong with her? Was this really happening? Had she finally lost her mind?

Every bird tweet, every leaf skittering across the school stoop, exploded like a thunderclap. Soon the racket grew so great Eilwen did not even hear it anymore – it was no longer processed. Her body had given up. She realized she was shivering: legs shaking, spine tingling. The sores on her back felt on fire.

Maybe she'd been wrong, was the last thing she thought before her vision faded for good (she blinked frantically to regain it, but could not). Maybe the snake *had* been an omen. Maybe the black ones *could* hurt you. What would Hal have said if he were here? She didn't know. Hal never got sick – not until the end.

She doubled over, retching. Was this *her* end?

She curled up on the ground by the truck. The last thing she remembered seeing before darkness took her were two golden flecks where the snake's eyes had been.

The snake watched in silence – watched as Eilwen hiccupped and shuddered into unconsciousness. Only after Eilwen had ceased moving did it venture from beneath the truck.

It approached her body, which lay drenched in sweat on the dusty ground, and flicked its tongue along her length. It nudged under her arm and found a warm spot beneath her chin, where her pulse and breath were strongest.

* * *

The woman who had come to see her was well-dressed.

She was slender and fair-haired, with odd eyes: gray, with flecks of green fighting to shine through. She appeared stern. Withdrawn. The nice lady had told Eilwen, though, that this woman had come just to see her. Just for Eilwen.

But as Eilwen studied the woman, with the all-absorbing eyes all three-year-olds share, she began to think differently. The nice lady had Eilwen by the hand, urging her to approach the woman, but Eilwen hung back, sensing the woman's unease.

"What's her name, again?" The woman's arms were folded over her chest, as though in case the toddler attacked.

"Eilwen," said the nice lady. She coaxed Eilwen forward again but Eilwen refused, anxiously entangling her free fist in her black hair.

"Beg pardon?" The woman's tone sharpened.

"Eil-wen. E-I-L-W-E-N. She'll respond to nothing else."

"Is that a real name? That's not a real name. Where's her birth certificate? Was it stored properly? Is the name smudged?"

"We have nothing on record. Few of the children here come with papers."

The woman sighed. Eilwen could hear every brisk breath she took, which emphasized the unnerving fact that her body never moved in time with her breathing. "I suppose it's for the best. Let me have her. We've got a long drive ahead."

"Very well, Ms. Sheehan."

"It's Mrs. Hittle now."

"Oh, congratulations!" The nice lady led Eilwen and the woman down a long hallway. Their footsteps echoed, their voices clanging off the metal pipes lining the ceiling. The sound waves were practically visible. The clamor grew the further they walked, the once-clean echoes blending into a wreckage of noise. Waves entangled, whirring between Eilwen's ears, ringing in her brain. Pulsing against the backs of her eyes. For a moment her unconscious mind equated the throbbing, scorching beat with the steady rhythm of the switch. She panicked and slipped her hand — suddenly sweaty — out of the nice lady's grip right before they reached the end of the hall. She tumbled backwards and screamed, for there was no floor beneath her, nothing to break her fall...

"Eilwen!" a panicked voice whispered.

Silence met her ears so suddenly it was like lightning zapped the world away.

Her eyes opened, then closed. She was awake, she realized.

"Eilwen," the voice repeated. "Are you with us? Can you breathe? Aunt Thelma, can she breathe? She started gasping."

Eilwen realized she was breathing heavily, though the rest of her body was still. Her eyes didn't even want to reopen. "I'm breathing," she managed to mumble.

"Thank the Good Lord." Eilwen heard Dristan take some deep breaths of his own. "How's your head? You still feel so hot. Eilwen, are you thirsty at all?"

Dristan's words did not register immediately. For all Eilwen knew, hours had passed between when she heard them and when she asked, voice a slur, "Where am I?" Her surroundings smelled odd. The air didn't move like it did outside, but scent told her she was not in the school building, the truck, or any room in the Homestead. She tried to open her eyes again and succeeded.

"You're at my aunt's home." Eilwen turned her head – which rested on a crocheted pillow – toward Dristan's worried voice. He was kneeling beside her. "Eilwen, what happened?"

"Leave her be, Dristan," came Thelma Duvall's voice from somewhere behind Eilwen. "Question her after she comes to."

Eilwen tried to think back to what had happened before the dream, which she already found herself forgetting. "I had a headache," she said. "How did I get here?"

"Gus found you on the ground with this *snake* beside you," Dristan explained, the strain in his voice suggesting he was suppressing disgust or panic. "I thought you'd been bitten, but then he starts telling me about the snake's head and how *somehow* that makes it harmless –"

"I checked you over, dear," Thelma interjected. She took a seat on a rickety piano stool so she could better face the sofa on which Eilwen lay. She was a pretty woman and looked very much like her nephew, blue eyes and all. "No bite marks. My theory's heatstroke. Dristan's mother told me he had a fit like this last summer right

60

before his birthday. It's always hotter in cities, especially with that devilish heat wave last year. Poor Dristan was sweating like a whore in church, and his house had air conditioning!"

"I asked Agnes if we could borrow her pony, and we heaved you onto it and brought you here," Dristan said. "Gus said he reckoned you should recover here instead of at the Homestead. Said your aunt's cussing a blue-streak over this. Something about there being a problem with you and a snake yesterday, too."

"*She's* the problem, not me or the snake," Eilwen snapped irritably, then apologized for her uncalled-for tone and closed her eyes again. "Thank you, Miss Thelma," she said, working to keep the slur from her voice. "I appreciate the help, ma'am. You and your nephew have been terribly kind."

"Oh hush, dear, I can hear the strain in your words." Thelma stood. "Dristan, now that we know she can wake up, let her sleep. That's what Cicely did with you, let you sleep it off. Seemed to work, didn't it?"

"Yeah. I'll bring a pitcher of water in so she has something to drink if she needs it. Can't hurt."

"It can if you break another one of my pitchers! Get her water, but don't rush, you clumsy thing. I'll fetch some linens in case the sweat chills her, but after that, let her be. The goats need milking anyway and you're still so terrible at it you need all the practice you can get."

Dristan smiled warmly at his aunt and nodded as she left the room. He reached down and stroked Eilwen's damp hairline. Startled, Eilwen jerked away. "Sorry," Dristan said. "Feel better, all right?"

61

Eilwen nodded, eyes still shut. "Can I ask you something?"

"Of course."

"Why'd you hurry to the creek at lunch like that?"

She opened her eyes in time to see surprise flash across his face. Followed by relief. "I imagine the same reason you were searching the ditch yesterday."

"I still don't know what that reason is," Eilwen admitted.

"Neither do I." As Dristan left the room, he added, "I know it's important, though."

Eilwen closed her eyes once more, allowing herself a feeling of relief for the simple fact that another human being understood the odd impulses that possessed her.

* * *

"If that silly girl fainted, it's her own fault. I need her home."

"I'm sorry, Mona," said Thelma. "She's still recovering. Poor thing's only slept on and off since Dristan brought her here."

"That's another thing I take issue with!" snapped Mona. She and Dale were at the end of the path leading from the road to Thelma's cottage. Mona was face-to-face with Thelma, her tone malicious. "That your pious papist brat took it upon himself to decide what happens to my charge! Where does that rat get off?"

"Mrs. Hittle, I will not have my family or my faith insulted on my own land!"

"You call this land? It's ten acres at most! The Hittles have farmed the same thousand for a century and a half!"

"Surely you can continue one afternoon without the aid of a sick girl!"

"She's faking it! I know she is! I'll go in there and prove it!" Mona pushed Thelma aside and shouted savagely at the cottage; Dale had to physically hold her back. "YOU HEAR ME, YOU LITTLE BRAT? I KNOW WHAT YOU'RE PULLING! EILWEN TABB, YOU GOD-DAMNED UNGRATEFUL BASTARD! YOUR WHORE MOTHER WOULD'VE DISOWNED YOU HERSELF IF SHE HADN'T DIED FIRST!"

"MONA!" Dale had to shout to be heard over his wife, who was near tears. "Let's go. We're wasting time. I'll pick Eilwen up tonight when she's rested."

"She'll have run away by then!"

"Where's she gonna go, Mona?" Dale shook his wife. "Where's she gonna run to 'round here?"

Mona sobbed once, then shut her eyes and appeared to hold her breath. It took a moment, but she settled down. She wiped her eyes and smoothed her bobbed strawberry-blond hair. "Very well," she said. "It's allergy season. I'm willing to admit the girl might be sick, even if she's being an exaggerating wimp about it." She allowed Dale to guide her from the pathway and down Lily Lane. Dale turned to mouth *I'm sorry* to Thelma when Mona couldn't see.

"Heaven above." Dristan was watching at the living room window, the lacy curtains casting a whimsical pattern across his face.

Eilwen peered over his shoulder. "What is it?"

Dristan looked at her. "Did you not hear all that?"

"What about it?"

Dristan looked ready to be appalled, then shook his head and looked back out the window. "Nothing. That's usual stuff to you, isn't it? That fit-throwing?"

Eilwen chortled. "That wasn't a fit." She grabbed a handful of cookies from the plate Thelma had left in the room. It was nice to be able to eat without fear of having your share either given to Gus or tossed to the hog if you didn't eat it fast enough, and Eilwen, out of habit, had stuffed her face for an embarrassingly long time before remembering she was a guest in another house. Still, that hadn't stopped her from enjoying being able to gorge herself. She was wiping crumbs from her mouth when she noticed Dristan staring at her. "What?"

"I just don't see the resemblance."

"Resemblance?"

"Between you and your aunt. Or your uncle. To which are you related?"

"Aunt. My mother was her older sister and ruined the Sheehan family name by having me out of wedlock," Eilwen explained, unprompted, as Mona used to have her recite this to every person she met. "Aunt says that's why she could never marry better than Uncle. That's why she hates me so much. That's why she never whips Gus. Well, *almost* never. I'm sorry, but is there any more food? I never realize I'm hungry 'til I eat."

Perhaps it was the food she could eat without fear, or the long nap on the sofa, but Eilwen had never felt as pleasant as she felt that afternoon. Both mind and body felt perplexingly healthy – rejuvenated. As though her fainting spell had kick-started a motor that had been dormant all her life. Maybe she really had been sick, she

64

considered as the day wore on. Maybe she'd been sick for years, and today was the first day she'd not been. Maybe she'd sweated it all out, and the reason she felt good now was just because she felt *normal*, for once, and had never known feeling good was possible. Never known she was sick. Never known she'd felt half awake, half aware and half full all her life. She'd been used to feeling all that. She'd assumed that was normal. That that was her default state.

But suddenly, this afternoon, she knew what she felt now was normal. What *should* be normal. This was her: this clear-headed, friend-having, cookie-eating Eilwen she'd never known existed. She worried how she was going to keep this Eilwen alive after returning to the Homestead.

"Did you feel this good after your heatstroke?" she asked Dristan that evening. They were sitting on the split-rail fence around the goat yard, eating apples. The breeze was fresh and the goats bleated as they grazed. Everything felt and smelled and sounded crystal clear, but not one bit overwhelming. Eilwen had never felt so at peace.

"I do remember feeling spectacular afterwards, oddly enough," Dristan said. "I was lucky. Lots of people were passing out from heat. We were always worrying they wouldn't wake up again. I was worried I wouldn't…

"When my dad got sick from the flood water, it was like that. Every time he shut his eyes, I was terrified it'd be the last time I saw them. Ended up being true one day. They never reopened."

Eilwen, unsure what to say, handed Dristan another apple.

"I'm just glad he went before Mom," Dristan said, taking the fruit. "It would've killed him worse if he'd had to see her die."

"Sounds like he loved her," Eilwen observed, as though this were unusual.

"More than anything. The last thing he told me was to take care of her. Protect her. She died a few months later. Broken heart, I know it. It's scary what love does to the body."

* * *

Thelma had lent Eilwen a dress for the afternoon, as Eilwen's clothes were drenched in sweat. Eilwen was used to wearing pants, having done so ever since she'd gotten good enough at sewing to alter the cheap jeans she saved up for every year, and so she felt odd wearing her boots and Hal's cap with the bright yellow dress hanging loosely on her form. Dristan had tried to comfort her by assuring her it complimented her eyes.

"I just don't like not being covered up down there when I work," she said, trying to explain why she had reserve about tromping after him into the woods, as he was insisting she do.

He had again displayed a spontaneous urge to flee into the trees. Immediately after dinner (during which Eilwen had made another spectacle of herself, shoveling down food as though it would be taken from her at any minute), Dristan had leapt up and declared he needed to find another creek.

"I don't even know of a creek nearby, except the one behind the Hittles'," Thelma had said. "And it don't run near us."

"Doesn't matter," Dristan had said. "I'll find it."

Thelma had shaken her head. "He's like a bloodhound when it comes to water. You can take the boy out of River City…"

Dristan had then led Eilwen to the edge of the woods by the goat yard. The sun was nearly set, the sky watery blue, fading purple in the east. Lightning bugs waltzed above the grass.

"You're sure a creek's back there?" Eilwen asked curiously, as Dristan worked to free his sleeve from a wild rose bush. Eilwen had never seen him so hurried. He was determined to find that creek.

"If not a creek, a stream," he said. "And if not a stream, an overflowing ditch. There's something."

"Is it an animal you're after?" Eilwen finally asked point-blank.

Dristan stopped moving. His eyes lingered on the trees, then fell on Eilwen. "May I tell you something?" Eilwen nodded. "That day last year, when I had my heatstroke, I was down by the river. I could always see it from my window, but I wanted to see it in person that day. I didn't know what was driving me, all I knew was I needed to be near water. The only reason I'm telling you this without fear of appearing insane is because I know you've felt that urge, too." He looked Eilwen deep in the eye, silently conveying both his desperation for someone who understood him and the melancholy joy of finally easing that desperation. "May not be regarding the same thing, but you've felt it, haven't you? That... *sudden pull* to do or find something, though you've got no earthly idea what it is, or why you must find it?"

Eilwen swallowed. It was difficult to address aloud what she'd been mulling over in silence for so long. What was it about words that made things realer? She nodded, thinking of the snake, but afraid to tell Dristan. He'd seemed repulsed by it earlier.

Dristan looked like he might laugh for joy. "I knew it. As soon as I saw you on the ground with that snake, I knew it!"

Eilwen's jaw dropped. "Knew what?" Did Dristan know what the snake meant?

"Right before I got sick that day, I saw an otter." Dristan apparently hoped Eilwen would catch on; he paused before sighing, "Am I right in assuming you saw the snake before your spell?"

"You're looking for your otter," Eilwen realized. "But you saw it all the way back in Louisville!"

"And I think she followed me."

Had Eilwen not experienced for herself her own pull toward an animal, she would have indeed thought Dristan mad. Instead, she empathized. Which made her fear for her own sanity. She tensed: it was dangerous to go mad on a farm.

Dristan looked longingly into the trees. "She was my friend. My secret pet. We swam together, fished together... I'd bring her scraps from dinner, she'd bring me presents she'd dived for in the river. She brought me a ring, once. I was closer to this otter – this wild animal – than I was to any of my human friends. For almost a year,

68

not a day passed I didn't see her. Not even snow stopped me." He licked his lips. "The flood did, though. I thought she'd been washed away. Her home was gone – the place on the bank where we'd met. All under water. I didn't think I'd see her again. Killed me inside."

Eilwen was disappointed when she imagined never seeing the snake again and realized it wouldn't "kill her inside". Maybe she hadn't felt the same tug. Maybe this wasn't the magical secret she'd looked forward to learning about. Agnes's words from yesterday played in her head: *You dream about fairies all the time and have yet to meet any.* Maybe that was her curse: getting glimpses – teasing hints – of something special, but never enjoying it herself. Be it fairies, magical animal friends, or a bed only her brother was allowed to have.

"But the other day, I sensed her. For the first time in months. God, maybe I am going insane." Dristan ran a hand through his brown locks. He looked pleadingly at Eilwen. "You do know what I'm talking about?"

"I do. I hope." Eilwen felt distressed. "What do you think this all means? The... *pull.* The animals. Is there something to it?"

"Has to be. Why else would it exist?"

"Plenty of things exist for no reason," said Eilwen gloomily.

"That's a sad thought."

Eilwen shrugged.

"Is something the matter?" Dristan asked. "You were feeling swell earlier."

Eilwen looked out across the field. "I don't want to leave." The evening breeze, the lightning bugs and stars, felt like a death sentence tonight.

"I'll see you tomorrow," Dristan promised encouragingly. "And we'll stay friends. We have to. No matter what that horrible aunt of yours says. In fact, stay here with us! For good! Aunt Thelma would love having you."

"I can't." When Dristan looked ready to argue, she explained, "The tobacco needs me."

Dristan looked almost angry. "Are you joking? The only reason you stay with those people is for some plant?"

"You think tobacco is like any other old crop?" Eilwen lashed. Then she softened: Dristan's shock clearly stated he hadn't meant to offend. "I guess you need to experience it to understand... Dristan, it's so much more than a plant. It's... magical too, somehow." Eilwen brightened when she realized there was indeed something in her life toward which she felt a *pull*. Something that would "kill her inside" to lose. "But even if it wasn't, I promised Old – a friend, I'd make certain it was looked after. And tobacco needs *lots* of looking after."

When Uncle Dale came for her not much later, Eilwen was forced to leave behind the first true haven she'd ever known outside the curing barn. That night, she dreamt again of the gray-walled building, and the woman who'd come to take her from it.

Chapter IV

Saving Grace

But you must have hope, and you must have faith,
You must love and be strong – and so—
If you work, if you wait, you will find the place
Where the four-leaf clovers grow.
– Ella Higginson, "Four-Leaf Clover"

The horse glared at Eilwen with fire in its eyes.

Eilwen glared cautiously back, mentally plotting her next move. It was difficult to think clearly when shaken from having a massive draft animal angrily charge you out of nowhere, but even so, Eilwen was thrilled to still be thinking clearly at all. She had worried it would wear off – that the fogginess that had plagued her all her life would return overnight, silently imprisoning her once more, suffocating her focus and drive.

But it hadn't.

Eilwen stepped toward the fence. Mahitabel snorted and stamped. Eilwen felt acutely the tremors through the earth.

Yes, the world still greeted her senses with crystal intensity. The only difference was that today, just as yesterday after waking from her spell, Eilwen's mind was suddenly able to handle it. To manage, sort and prioritize every sensation – every texture of sound, every color of smell... But sacrificing no vibrancy.

Today, Eilwen had woken feeling invincible. Especially because Mona had been particularly un-mean since last night. Likely she feared anyone at school talking about yesterday's events more than necessary.

So Mona's vengeance had been subtle: "Seeing as how you're *recovering*," she'd hissed the word, "your job this morning is bringing Hitty in. Your uncle put her out to pasture and now she's acting jumpy. Just get her in her stall so we can look her over."

Eilwen had entered Mahitabel's field only to be violently charged. A hoof had scraped her boot as she'd scrambled between fence rails to escape.

Mahitabel whinnied piercingly and Eilwen cupped her ears. She had hoped to run into the snake again, but Mahitabel seemed fitful over more than something she might have spotted on the ground. She hated *Eilwen* right now. She wanted *Eilwen* dead. The draft horse gave a growly bray, charged the fence, then waltzed backwards, head bobbing. Eilwen removed Hal's cap and ran a hand through her hair.

Rope. There was rope in the barn. Even if Mahitabel didn't let Eilwen near enough to halter, it would be a victory just getting rope around her neck.

Eilwen sped through the grass toward the animal barn. The chickens clucked skittishly as she passed, but she paid them no heed as she searched for rope. Mona had given her a task so threateningly simple the consequence for failure had to be severe.

A barn cat watched with orange eyes as Eilwen gathered what rope she could find. The chickens' nervous clucking had evolved into a terrified uproar by the time Eilwen exited the barn, attempting to tie multiple scraps of rope together. She stopped and watched the clamoring birds.

For some reason – some odd reason that emerged from nowhere – she couldn't shake the feeling that she was being watched, and wondered if the chickens, sensitive as they were, felt the same. It was the same feeling she'd had two days ago, when she thought she'd seen a pair of eyes watching her from the woods: luminous but rusty eyes the same shape as the blackberry leaves. Against her will, she made herself return to the horse's field, wading through the tall grass.

She was just trying to convince herself that her overactive imagination was a result of her high sensitivity to everything when she suddenly found herself face-to-face with a big black snake.

Eilwen dropped the rope, sucked in air, but did not scream.

It had come out of nowhere. The black head was at eye level with her, inches from her face. Most of its long body lifted off the ground. It was motionless. Not swaying or shivering to strike. Eilwen may as well have stumbled upon a statue of a serpent out in the middle of the field.

Eilwen, too, was motionless – frozen where she stood, upper body instinctively leaning away from the snake. Yet her gaze instinctively found its familiar yellow eyes. The world seemed to disappear. All she could think about was the snake – that it was here, in her field, literally face-to-face with her.

And it was not a dream.

Was it?

Remembering to exhale, Eilwen struggled to breathe evenly as she slowly straightened her stance. Once straight, she blinked, and was shocked when she thought she saw the snake blink too.

"Huh…" she said dumbly, her inner argument with herself about whether this was a dream gaining strength. She cocked her head, and the snake mimicked her.

Eilwen's mouth went dry. This was it: what she'd been waiting for, for four years. All her dreams about lonely black serpents lost in the woods, searching endlessly, sometimes braving the depths of lakes and rivers, sometimes gliding through the air as though on wings… but searching, always searching. Not one of those dreams had brought fear, despair, or reptilian ire. They had only brought hope and peace and, despite the lost-ness the snake felt, a sense of clarity – of the world being on its way to making sense for the first time. The reassurance the dreams had brought her always ended upon waking, but while she had them, they were the closest Eilwen felt to feeling loved since Old Hal.

Eilwen un-tilted her head. The snake kept its angled, flickering a purple forked tongue. Eilwen, observing the snake's velvet black scales in sunlight for the first time, decided irrevocably that she had never seen a creature so beautiful. She licked her lips, then stammeringly told it, "It's nice to see you up close."

The snake flicked its tongue again, then relaxed, its body resembling a gracefully arched swan neck.

Suddenly it moved – lurched forward, head inches from Eilwen's hand. Eilwen gasped, but then, without hesitation, stroked its head as one would a purring kitten. Like a kitten, the snake pushed its head up into her hand. Eilwen felt an urge to laugh.

How odd this was! The snake continued to rub against her: sometimes hesitantly as though gauging Eilwen's character, sometimes confidently as though it and Eilwen had known each other since birth. It circled her; sniffed her with its tongue; raised and lowered its body as if trying to look Eilwen up and down; nuzzled affectionately against her. The more Eilwen touched the creature, the more she felt herself loving it. It was instantaneous and gradual. Powerful and delicate. Eilwen wondered again if this was the *pull* Dristan was talking about, and this time her answer was a confident *Yes*. Dristan and his otter had had over a year to know each other – of course losing her had crushed him! Eilwen had only been gingerly petting this snake a few minutes, but already never wanted to be another day without it.

The snake followed her around the farm the rest of the day with both the loyalty of a dog and the unpredictability of a cat. It did not like loud noises or sudden movement, and its loyalty died when Eilwen drew near any cows or other larger animals, whose presence sent it shooting up trees or slipping away into the grass or cornstalks. Eilwen was grateful for the snake's timidity though: nothing good could come of Mona finding it. Mona discovering its importance to Eilwen would mean its death, whether it was one of the rat-eating snakes or not.

But no matter who was near, the snake was never more than a stone's throw away. Right before lunch, Eilwen feared Dale would notice it hiding in a gutter above where he'd chosen to take a heat break. When he asked what was wrong, Eilwen, who'd been nervously wringing her cap, lied that she felt faint again. Dale sighed and told her to sit in some shade, and the snake, surreptitiously slipping down the rainspout, joined her seconds later.

"Dristan gave his otter a name," Eilwen thought aloud as she and the snake walked and slithered a path through the front yard. The oaks' shade camouflaged the snake, which put Eilwen at ease; she thought she'd spotted Mona behind the living room curtain. "Is it okay if I give you one? I don't wanna just call you Snake. Unless you'd like it."

The snake stopped slithering and shook its head.

Eilwen didn't know whether to rub her eyes.

The path ended where the driveway met Bloomfield Road. Tucked in the corner was the beginning of a stone-lined ditch about three feet deep, randomly angled, with stone steps at every other bend. It was ancient and smooth, coated in moss and lichens. The long leaves of ditch lilies lined the structure, providing privacy if one crouched down. "Hal told me he helped his father build this," Eilwen said to the snake, who zipped ahead into the stonework as a child races toward a playground. It investigated every nook and cranny. Eilwen took a seat on a step and watched until the snake grew bored and returned to her. "It used to be a drainage ditch, but dirt floated away when it rained, so they lined it with its own creek rock. Creek's not here anymore, but they couldn't get rid of the lilies. Hal said it's because fairies live in them."

She rubbed the snake's head with a finger, and it lifted, liking it. "You can live in here, if you like. It's damp, got tons of mice – the corn cellar's nearby. And it's got the lilies you like. That was you in the ditch the other day, wasn't it? When I was walking home from school?"

The snake flicked its tongue. Eilwen smiled. There was definitely something special about this snake. Something magical.

"Can I call you Gracie?"

The snake flicked its tongue again.

"You are a girl, aren't you?"

Another tongue flick.

"Of course you are. You're a big snake. Boys don't get this big."

Gracie shook her head again.

Eilwen hummed another laugh and smiled more widely than she had in years. Yes, she thought. Definitely something magical.

"I need to go in for lunch," she told the snake reluctantly after some time. She straightened her cap, thought a moment, then removed it. "Here." She set it on the cool stone floor. "My head should've warmed it."

Gracie coiled inside the cap as much as she could. Half her long body lay outside it, but she looked content.

"I'll be back soon," Eilwen promised her. "I swear. Just stay in here for now, okay?"

Eilwen had difficulty leaving the ditch. Several times she walked halfway to the house before changing her mind and turning back, only to scold herself and march determinedly toward the porch again. When she finally made it, she yanked open the door and shut it swiftly behind her with half a mind to lock it.

"What's so fascinating out front?"

Mona had her back to Eilwen, stirring a pot over the fire, but she had asked the question the instant Eilwen appeared in the kitchen doorway.

Eilwen swallowed. "I wasn't feeling good."

"What made you go to the front yard to recover?"

"Leaves," Eilwen lied stiffly. "Hal and I used to… count leaves."

Gus entering through the side door spared her from further interrogation. He had Shep with him, and was wiping his sweaty head with a rag Mona was not thrilled about him using.

"That's what your shirt's for!" She snatched the rag from him and flung it angrily into the corner. "If Eilwen weren't so evil, you'd do the laundry yourself!"

"Thanks for being so evil, Eilwen," Gus whispered as he sat by her at the table.

Eilwen shrugged sarcastically. "I do what I can."

"Feelin' all right? Uncle told me you were faint."

"She's still *recovering*," spat Mona.

Eilwen folded her hands, smiled tiredly, and nodded toward Mona as an answer.

"I meant to tell you," Gus said. "Dristan came looking for you."

"What?" said Eilwen alertly.

"You were out in the field with Hitty."

"What'd he say?"

"Probably wants to finish converting her." Mona dropped two plates of gravy-slathered food on the table, making sure Eilwen's landed messily. "You're cleaning that up."

Gus waited for Mona to return to the pot. "He said he found something he wants you to see. He was real excited."

Eilwen drummed her fingers, mind racing. "He didn't say what it was?"

"Wouldn't tell me. Are you in love? Did you kiss yesterday?"

"No!" Eilwen said more loudly than she'd intended. Mona whipped around to glare at her.

"'Cause that's what everyone at school thinks now," Gus whispered. "Since you two spent the rest of the day alone together."

Eilwen slouched and bit back a moan. "All the other girls *clearly* fancy him... And we weren't alone, his aunt was there!"

"I don't want any more talk of that boy in this house," declared Mona. She left the pot simmering, dusted her hands, and fixed herself a plate, which she soaked in gravy – the only way to tolerate the gamy bacon that was the last of the meat from last year's hog slaughter. "And Eilwen, you're not to see him anymore. Or talk to him again. Understood? Gus, if he comes calling for her again, you're to send him on his way and tell him we don't tolerate papists on our property. Understood?"

Gus opened his mouth in protest, but then cast Eilwen a look that said *I'm sorry*. "Yes, Aunt."

Eilwen hardly ate, appetite suddenly gone. Her stomach hurt.

As soon as she stepped outside, Gracie came racing to her like a bolt of black lightning. She slithered up Eilwen's leg and draped across her shoulders, nuzzling her cheek.

Eilwen realized she was suddenly more grateful than sad; Gracie's presence alone eased the stomachache she'd fought during lunch. "I really *am* evil," she chuckled as Gracie looped through the waves in her ponytail.

Gracie must have disagreed, for she fell to the ground and slithered away. Seconds later, Eilwen heard footsteps. Minutes later, Uncle Dale appeared around the corner of the animal barn. "That Dristan boy's here to see you," he told her.

Eilwen stiffened. Uncle Dale hadn't been present for Mona's latest proclamation. She paused only long enough to consider if she could get away with this. "Where is he?"

"Told him to wait in the barn." Dale wiped his sunbeaten face with his overalls. He was so red anymore his freckles were hardly visible. "How was it getting Hitty in? She behave?"

Eilwen paused again. The rope she'd been going to use to accomplish that task was probably still in the field where she'd dropped it. "I…"

"Because she's calmed down since you put her back. I was wonderin' how you did it. Haven't seen her this cool since Sunday."

Eilwen paused yet again. "I… So she's in the barn?" She added hastily, "Still?"

Dale nodded, looking shocked and impressed. "I really thought she'd kill you this morning. I'll be honest though, this ain't the first time you've proved me wrong."

Dale proceeded toward the house, gently shoving Eilwen toward the barn entrance as he passed her. After he disappeared into the house, Eilwen hesitated, gathering her thoughts, then sprinted into the barn.

"Dristan?" Eilwen spotted the Louisvillian at Mahitabel's stall, speaking softly to her. The massive horse, whose head alone was the length of Dristan's arm, watched the boy with sleepy eyes. Dristan certainly had a calming aura about him.

He turned at his name, his eyes bright blue even in the dark of the barn. "Eilwen! I'm so glad! How are you feeling today?"

"Decent," she replied distractedly as she approached the stall, studying Mahitabel. "Better than yesterday."

Dristan didn't hesitate. "Any luck with the snake?"

Neither did Eilwen. "Show me what you want to show me first."

Dristan grinned.

"She's outside." He grabbed Eilwen's hand (ignorant of her flinching gasp) and led her out of the barn, turning so they were behind it, on the side facing the fields and away from the house. Loose bales of hay, green with seedlings, were piled here. Dristan rolled up the sleeves of his jacket and lifted some of the hay.

A furry brown otter emerged. It gazed at Dristan adoringly as it waddled toward him and paused at his feet. When the otter realized a third party was present, it rested its cerulean eyes on Eilwen, whose heart caught in her throat – for now she understood more than ever. This was Dristan's snake. His Gracie.

"Isn't she beautiful?" Eilwen thought she saw tears in Dristan's eyes. "I knew she'd find me. I don't know how."

"She's gorgeous," Eilwen agreed.

Dristan held the otter in his arms. "I've named her Cicely."

"After your mother," Eilwen said.

Dristan smiled at her, flattered she remembered. "Now I can keep my promise to Dad, and take care of her."

He sat on the hay and held Cicely in his lap, petting her, loving her, Cicely returning the affection tenfold. Eilwen watched as the boy before her reconnected, after months of what must have been bitter grief-filled loneliness, with the one part of his life that had survived the flood. The one part not destroyed, diseased, or carried off by angry water. It finally hit Eilwen that Dristan McAtee had lost everything. His family. His house. Every possession he'd ever owned… even his town. The life into which he'd been born more than uprooted: the very soil into which his roots once delved had been washed away as well.

And until today, he'd thought he'd also lost his otter. This secret little friend had survived the flood just to find him again. Eilwen sat slowly beside him. "Where did you find her?"

Dristan lifted Cicely's long but plump body and planted a kiss on her nose. She trilled. "I felt the pull again this morning. Ran into the woods – didn't even eat – and searched the trees. It took forever, but I found the creek, and as soon as I did, she found me."

Eilwen said wistfully, "She has your eyes."

Dristan beamed. He then nodded at something behind Eilwen's shoulder. "That snake has your eyes."

Eilwen spun around. Sure enough, there was Gracie. Old Hal's cap dangled awkwardly from her mouth. Eilwen's spirit soared. "You're a sneaky thing…"

Dristan laughed, "So you found yours too!"

"She found me." Gracie looped around Eilwen's neck. The cap dropped in her lap and Eilwen placed it back on her head. "In the field this morning."

They sat in the hay in blissful silence, the emotions they felt too dear for words. There was no need to channel and limit them with language, mostly because they had no words for what they felt. And though somewhere in the backs of their minds they wondered painstakingly about the logical reasons behind this inexplicable connection they felt with wild animals, they were too relieved – too excited and happy – to care for reasons right now. Right now, all that mattered was that the animals were there at all.

Gracie had settled sleepily in the crook of Eilwen's elbow. "By the way," Eilwen said at long last, the first either had spoken in a while, "Dristan, thank you for bringing Hitty in. Gracie distracted me."

"Um, well… You're welcome. But I don't know who Hitty is."

"The horse you were talking to in the barn."

Dristan stared at her concernedly. "I didn't bring the horse anywhere. She was in the stall when I got here."

Eilwen searched his face for signs of jest, or pranking. She'd seen other children pull this sort of thing with each other, but this was her first personal experience. "What do you mean?"

"Exactly what I said."

"How –? Then who –?"

"EILWEN MARGARET TABB!"

Mona's voice carried across the side-yard.

Eilwen's bones turned to jelly. "Dristan, you need to go! Right now!"

Gracie, sensing Eilwen's panic, slithered out of her arms and into the hay. "What are you in trouble for *now*?" Dristan demanded, staring in the direction of Mona's voice.

"I'm not supposed to see you anymore. Ever. Now go on!"

"Even at school?"

"I don't know, Aunt never thinks these things through..."

"WHERE ARE YOU!" Mona was inside the barn. "YOU SHOW YOUR ROTTEN LYING FACE!"

"GO, Dristan, NOW!" Eilwen hissed. "And remember, if anyone asks, I sent you away earlier!"

Anger flared in Dristan's eyes. Biting his lip, he grabbed Cicely and took off, circling around the barn on the side opposite Mona's approaching footsteps. Eilwen allowed herself a sigh of relief, but Mona was soon behind her.

Smack!

Eilwen fell face-first into the hay, the back of her head throbbing.

"You defiant little brat!" Mona's hand jerked back for another hit. Eilwen scrambled out of the hay and ducked just in time.

"Please, I sent him away!"

"After I just told you! After I just told you not to see him again! You sneak back here –"

"I told you, I sent him away!"

"– and lied to your uncle! Right to his face!" Mona hit Eilwen again. Eilwen wobbled, but before she could find her balance, she felt her arm seized. Mona's grip was like iron. "Get me the switch, Dale."

Uncle Dale had just caught up to his wife. "Mona, she's –"

"*Now!*"

Eilwen's face was hot with fear as she watched Dale lumber away. For the first time, she struggled to free herself. "Let me go!"

"Settle down!" Mona jerked her. "You brought this on yourself!"

"I sent him away! I did!" Eilwen pulled until her arm ached, then used her free hand to try prying off Mona's fingers.

"Stop that!" Mona spun around to hold Eilwen's other arm. "Hold still, damn it!"

Eilwen couldn't stop struggling. She wouldn't. She'd already started. She and Mona were practically wrestling each other to the ground when Mona, slightly panicked, shouted, "Hurry, Dale!"

Dale reappeared with the switch at a reluctant pace, then saw his wife struggling to hold down her niece, and ran. He'd been about to toss the switch to Mona when he stopped suddenly and belted, "Get it off! Get it off me! GAH!"

"What in God's name?" Mona looked up for a second to see what had happened – long enough for Eilwen to wrench an arm free. "Damn it, Dale, help me!"

"It won't leave me alone!"

"The Hell are you talking abo –?"

Mona gasped when she saw the long black snake attacking her husband's ankles.

Gracie struck repeatedly at Dale's legs. Her teeth never penetrated his denim overalls, but her aggressiveness kept him dancing. He stomped his feet, trying to crush her.

"NO!" Eilwen wailed.

"Dale, take Eilwen!" Mona ordered.

Dale maneuvered close enough to grab Eilwen's arm from Mona, still trying to crush Gracie. Eilwen, terrified for Gracie's safety, had stopped fighting.

Mona slowly raised her thin figure off the ground. Her white dress was soiled, her stockings ripped, revealing long slits of her bony legs. "That damn snake," she hissed. Weeds and hay fell from her hair. "I've had all I can stand of it. This ends *now*."

Like rusted metal, Mona, despite her haggard appearance, was perfectly composed as she walked calmly into the animal barn, retrieved a hoe, and returned with it gripped in the telltale fashion of one about to destroy a snake.

Eilwen's blood turned to ice. "NO! No, Aunt, I'll be good! I'll stop fighting!" Despite her words, Eilwen began struggling more than ever to free herself. But Dale was stronger than Mona; if Mona's grip had been iron, Dale's was solid steel. "Please, Aunt Mona, I'll let you whip me, just don't hurt her! Don't hurt her, *please!*"

"Killing this wretched thing should be punishment enough, but if you want a whipping afterwards, we'll oblige." Mona neared Dale, whose ankles Gracie still valiantly battled.

"Go, Gracie!" Eilwen shouted. "Damn it, just leave! *Go!*" She reached down to grab her, but Dale held her up.

Eilwen burst into tears. She kicked and thrashed, but Mona was inches from Gracie, poised to strike…

The wind picked up.

It roared suddenly. The gust, not unlike a small tornado, thrust them all to the ground. Eilwen grunted as Dale fell on her, but she scrambled free, unaffected by the swirling wind. She didn't stop to question it: she grabbed Gracie and raced for the tobacco fields, not looking back.

Her face was streaked with tears when she reached the edge of the nearest field and bolted inside. The giant golden leaves that brushed her as she moved seemed to be trying to wipe them away. Clutching Gracie, she ran for what felt like hours, never leaving the sanctuary of the tobacco.

When she could run no longer, she dropped to the ground between two furrows, breathed heavily, and wept.

* * *

She would never tend Hal's tobacco again.

The thought tortured her as she traced the vein of a leaf. Mona would not punish her after today. Mona would go straight for disownment. She'd always wanted to. This just gave her an excuse. Eilwen would be sent to an orphanage. A crowded, miserable, metal orphanage, surrounded by other miserable orphans whose parents weren't even dead – just poor.

The sun was low. The tobacco leaves glowed yellow-green. Eilwen lay on her back, gazing at the giant leaves that shaded her, eyes sore from crying.

Her stomach gurgled. Gracie, who was laying on it, lifted her head.

"I don't know what to do," Eilwen admitted out loud.

Truthfully, she didn't know what it was that she didn't know what to do about. Was she *really* banned from the Homestead? Would it *really* mean the end if she tried to go back? Experience told her it would. Eilwen would be sleeping out here tonight.

She considered going to Dristan, but he had suffered enough. She didn't want to drag him into her suffering any more than she already had. No doubt Mona was over there harassing him and his aunt right now, demanding to know where she was. Eilwen herself wasn't quite sure where she was – which field she was in.

She felt sick. She had promised Hal she could take care of his tobacco when he was gone. The thought of living in the woods like a hermit, emerging only to pluck hornworms by moonlight, was crushing. What would she survive on? What would she do if she fell ill, or got hurt? With a sinking heart, Eilwen realized what she had to do. She would return to the Homestead, hat in hand, and beg forgiveness. Perhaps reminding Mona how few farmhands she had would save her. Free labor was the only thing Eilwen had to offer.

She stood, leaves sliding around her. "Come on, Gracie."

By the time they found their way out of the tobacco, the sun was nearly set. It was dark enough that Eilwen didn't fear being spotted as she made her way toward the curing barn. Atop the hill behind it, the single oak stood against a starry sky, the woods beyond a sea of blackening green. Eilwen choked as she approached the trees, for she could hear Gracie loyally following.

Eilwen stopped at the edge of the woods and looked down at Gracie. "You need to stay here."

Her voice shook as she spoke to the snake, who looked innocently at her. Eilwen shut her eyes and began walking toward the Homestead.

She sighed when she heard Gracie's slither in the grass. "No, Gracie." Eilwen pointed at the trees. "You can't come back with me."

Gracie flicked her tongue.

Eilwen's eyes burned. She held her face in her hands. Not wanting to suffer any more tears, Eilwen scooped up the snake, mentally repeating that this was for Gracie's safety. She stepped into the trees, placed her on the ground and prepared to tell her she never wanted to see her again… but the words wouldn't form. Each time she tried, they stuck in her throat and turned to sobs.

Eilwen fell to the ground in tears. Gracie watched confusedly, unsure what Eilwen wanted. Eilwen groaned loudly, sick and tired of crying – sick of tears and heartache and fear and confusion. Clawing her eyes, she cussed, kicked a few tree trunks, then stormed back out under the oak. Gracie watched from between two blackberry canes as Eilwen dropped to the ground once more.

She curled up in the grass. Gracie raced to her. "I wish I knew what this all meant," Eilwen whispered, feeling utterly lost. "I wish I knew what you meant, Gracie. I wish I knew why I love you." Could love exist for no reason?

Gracie, having no words for comfort, nuzzled Eilwen's cheek, then slithered onto Eilwen's side and snuggled into the developing curve above her hip. The red western sky darkened. But just as Gracie's tail lifted out of the grass, it touched a bit of green that, illuminated by the last ray of sun, caught Eilwen's eye.

A four-leaf clover.

She sat up, causing Gracie to slide off. Heart racing, Eilwen lowered her head.

This couldn't be, could it? Four years of daily searching, and she'd found it by accident? Panicking, Eilwen counted to make sure there were, indeed, four leaves. Four whole leaves – not three with one split down the middle, or one clover layered deceivingly over another. There were so many ways to be fooled. So many ways to get your hopes up. But her breath caught. The four were there. Four entire leaves. On one stem.

Carefully, like handling a tobacco seedling, Eilwen plucked the clover. She felt a bittersweet joy as she remembered that the last time she'd seen one, she'd been sitting in Old Hal's lap.

Gracie examined the clover, flicking her tongue over it, and Eilwen smiled, feeling closer to the best friend she'd lost than she'd felt in four years. "Two *good* things came out of today," she whispered, sniffling. "I finally met you, Grace." Eilwen twirled the clover between her thumb and forefinger, as she remembered Hal once doing. "And now I can see fairies."

Gracie slithered into her lap. Eilwen, accepting that she would be spending the night outside, leaned against the oak trunk. She stroked Gracie's velvet scales and stared sleepily at the woods. This time, when she spied two burnt-orange eyes staring back, there was a face and pair of shoulders with them.

Eilwen blinked. But the face did not disappear. She sat up. "Who's there?"

She heard nothing, but saw someone move behind the blackberry briars. The person jerked downward. "Dristan?" she asked, though she knew it wasn't. The eyes were wrong. "Wh-who are you?"

The rusty eyes widened, glanced away, then rested on Eilwen. "You can *see* me?" a voice asked incredulously.

Chapter V

Familiarity

Come away, O human child!
To the waters and the wild
With a faery, hand in hand,
For the world's more full of weeping than you can understand.
– William Butler Yeats, "The Stolen Child"

Childlike excitement jolted through Eilwen. But as usual, she was afraid to get her hopes up. Was she dreaming? But the voice had sounded real; she had felt the air that carried it.

But she was at the end of a long, confusing day. Her mind was worn, possibly playing tricks. Eilwen had just convinced herself she had, indeed, imagined the voice when Gracie rose suddenly and stared at the trees. And it was then Eilwen could no longer deny that she could see the palely lit outline of a mysterious stranger within the darkening green.

The childlike excitement returned full speed. *A fairy!* her mind and heart screamed. Her mouth went dry. She clutched her clover, afraid to move. Afraid to breathe. This was the closest she'd ever been to magic being real, and though part of her feared it would end in disappointment, the other part wanted it to last as long as she could let it.

But what if it *was* real? What if it *was* a fairy? Gracie had been real, after all. And there was magic in her. There had to be.

Eilwen swallowed, heart pounding, and found her voice. "Yes," she said warily, almost breathlessly. "I can see you."

She heard an angry-sounding whisper, but couldn't make out the words. Louder, the voice asked, "How 'bout now?"

Eilwen felt goose-bumps all over her body. Was she excited or scared? Either way, she noticed no change – she could still see this person, whoever they were, in the leafy shadows. "Yes."

"Damn it!"

The voice cracked slightly.

Heart sinking, Eilwen wondered if it was one of her schoolmates. "If this is one of the Ruckriegal boys, I'll slug you!" she threatened, hoping she sounded more alert than she felt. Her anger stemmed more from disappointment than feeling trespassed on.

"What's a 'ruckriegal'?" the voice asked obliviously, as though Eilwen's threat had gone unheard. "Is that another language?"

Eilwen blinked. What was going on? Who was this person? She wanted to be excited – relieved that whoever this was seemed ignorant of the families around these parts, and thus must be more than human. It was too much of a coincidence: finding the clover, and then all of a sudden being able to see someone in the trees – the trees Eilwen had always wanted to believe held something magical. The trees in which Old Hal himself had once seen fairies. "Who are you?" Eilwen asked cautiously, careful not to allow her gaze to lose focus on the outline of the stranger's shoulders. "What are you doing here, what do you want?"

"Is it German? It sounds German." The boy – for it was indeed a young boy, Eilwen realized the longer she stared – moved his head forward, peering at her between the blackberry canes. "I'm just checking on you."

His eyes – dark, rusty orange – looked Eilwen over, then widened expectantly, and Eilwen realized he was awaiting her response.

"Oh. I…" Her mouth went dry again. All she could think to say was dumbly repeating, "Checking on me?"

"I am."

"How come?"

"You were sad." Eilwen's silence prompted the boy further. "I saw you earlier." There was a curious lilt to his words. "You were crying."

Eilwen's hands instinctively found Gracie.

Branches rustled suddenly, and the boy stepped forward. He ducked beneath the blackberry canes and rose again on the other side, further out of the woods but still enough within the bracken that he might sprint back into the trees at a moment's notice. Eilwen felt as though she were being approached by a curious fawn.

His big gawking eyes never left her. His head tilted as he studied her; his stance and behavior reminded Eilwen of the strong but cautious curiosity of a cat. But no matter what other animals he brought to mind, he appeared, at least physically, entirely human. No wings. No pointed ears or glowing eyes. His hair was red, but that was the only thing even remotely unusual about him.

He blinked, for the first time in what seemed like ages, and gave a slightly awkward closed-mouthed smile. But it was genuine. Warm. His face was young and handsome; it lowered as he bowed. "My name is Conor," he said.

Eilwen held Gracie – a bundle of coils – against her chest, as a nervous child clings to a doll.

Conor rose from his bow, smiling but hesitant about it; and Eilwen, nervous as she was, realized then that, of the two of them, this boy seemed to be the one who viewed *her* as the skittish animal. When he began stepping forward again his movements were lithe and graceful and, most importantly, quiet. Slow. He emerged completely from the trees and bracken with patience and great care for gradualness. He paused when he entered beneath the branches of the oak, standing a few feet from where Eilwen sat. "That's an awfully well-trained snake you've got there."

Eilwen, too stunned to speak, held Gracie tighter and nodded.

"Has she a name?" The lilt to his words was intriguing; the softest of accents, yet enough for even Eilwen's unworldly ear to know it was Irish.

Perhaps he was an immigrant, lost in the woods and surviving on what he could catch or steal for himself. That would explain his clothes: a loose cotton shirt beneath what looked like a fitted but very worn leather tunic. His boots were like Eilwen's, but that was the only modern-looking thing about him. He even carried a small, sheathed knife on his belt.

Was he here to rob her?

Or worse?

He must have somehow sensed her panic, despite the fact that Eilwen remained still as stone. He knelt slowly, lowering himself to eye level with her.

Eilwen nodded again. "Gracie."

Gracie hissed.

"There's a good name." Conor looked fondly at the snake, who slipped from Eilwen's grasp and coiled in striking position at her feet. Conor cleared his throat and backed up an inch. "I envy the ones who find each other last minute. Mine found me at three years, and I sure could've thought of some better names had I been a wee older. But then she's thinking the same thing about me, now, isn't she?"

He apparently expected Eilwen to laugh. He glanced down when she didn't. His eyes fell on her right hand. "Ah, so that's what did it. You didn't say you had a clover!"

Eilwen hid the clover protectively behind her back. "Should I have?" she asked worriedly.

"Oh, you owed me no such warning, no worries at all." Conor raised his hands and shook his head, his expression reassuring and exaggeratedly flippant; Eilwen nearly felt herself smile. But Gracie's defensiveness kept her guarded. "It's mighty relievin', actually. You see, I worried I was doing a terrible job concealing myself. But if it were a clover what let ya see me, then I've nothing to fret over." His smile was bright and cheerful. When Eilwen still responded with silence, he said, "You do know what it is a clover does, then, don't you?"

"It lets you see fairies." Eilwen's voice sounded even to herself as though she were in a dream.

96

Conor smiled again. "Someone taught ya well. Did they also mention they let you see through enchantments? Temporarily, at least."

Eilwen shook her head.

"It's true. And you saw through mine just now. I'm still only learning to cloak myself completely to human eyes, but I'm not too bad at it. I feared you saw me the other night when you were gathering firewood. That would've been my own fault. It was so dark out then I wasn't trying so hard as I should've to hide from ya. I gave the spell my all tonight, though. And damn if your clover didn't cut right through it!"

He laughed, and Eilwen smiled. Completely in awe. Wonderfully overwhelmed.

Still at a loss for words.

Finally, she managed, ineloquently, "Are you a fairy?"

Conor's smile widened. But he shook his head. "I'm not." He went from kneeling to sitting cross-legged. Gracie, glaring at him, flicked the tip of her tail against the oak leaves on the ground, mimicking the sound of a rattle. "Oh, hush, you."

Eilwen sat up. "Don't talk to her like that!"

Gracie hissed menacingly in agreement.

Conor looked apologetic. "I'm sorry. I didn't mean – it's just that for a while now, she's been –" He stopped midsentence and rubbed the back of his neck.

"I'm sorry," said Eilwen. She scooped up Gracie, who struggled to attack Conor's boots. "I don't mean to snap. I'm just tired and – Gracie, hold still! – tired and hungry, and already so confused."

"Confused about what?" Conor sounded interested.

Eilwen glanced unconsciously at Gracie. Conor made a thoughtful noise. "I reckon I must be confusing the hell out of ya too right now, am I right?"

Eilwen thought it would be rude to respond in the positive, so she remained silent.

"I'm sorry." Conor stood. "I assumed you knew more than ya did. If I may, how much *do* you know?"

Eilwen looked up at him, suddenly terrified he was going to leave. She wanted him to stay. Whatever – *who*ever – he was, it was special. Something to do with Gracie. Perhaps something to do with much, much more.

Eilwen realized her gut was telling her something. Some feeling deep inside was telling her – flat-out informing her – that tonight, right now, what was happening was meant to happen. Conor may not be a fairy, but Eilwen had never felt surer of anything in her life than that he was something important. And Old Hal had told her to trust her gut, hadn't he?

Instead of answering Conor's question, Eilwen asked, with suppressed excitement, "Did you say you were casting a *spell*?"

Conor tilted his head.

"You said my clover cut through your spell."

"Ah! Just an invisibility spell. Basic magic. But that particular spell's really hard to grasp right away. Takes months of practice and I've only been at it a few weeks. But I'm getting the hang of it," he added hastily, as though trying to impress her.

"So you can do magic?" Eilwen scrambled to her feet, never moving eyes, wide with wonder, from the magical stranger before her. "Magic is real?"

"Of course it is!" Conor shrugged and made a *Tuh!* sound. "And why wouldn't it be?"

"I don't…" Eilwen felt ashamed. Had she disappointed Hal by not adamantly believing in magic all these years? What was he thinking of her right now, looking down from Heaven? "I don't know."

"You really don't know anything, then, do you? I'm sorry, that sounded worse than I – What I meant was, you don't know what it is you should be knowing by now. Considering what you are."

"What I am?"

"And no wonder you're so tired, what with all the iron you're forced to work with on mundane farmsteads. I reckon you're tired all the time, aren't ya? Can't focus? Get frustrated and impatient real easy?"

Conor's spot-on summation of everything Eilwen had ever struggled with all her life alarmed her. "How did you –?"

"You aren't the only one." He studied her face amusedly. "But no matter how long you've been sufferin', it's better we find you now than later. Before it gets so confusing you go mad. I've heard horror stories of such things. I'd hate to see it happen to you, now."

"Who's *we*?" Eilwen asked.

"That's mighty hard to explain to someone who doesn't know anything about what they're supposed to know about." Conor rubbed the back of his head, looking like he was thinking very hard. He let his arm fall to his side and nodded toward the woods. "Come on. I'll show you."

He turned and stepped back into the bracken on the woods' edge. Eilwen remained under the oak tree. When Conor looked back at her, she asked, "In there?"

Conor nodded encouragingly. "In here."

Eilwen's thoughts raced but she was unable to process any of them. The only thing she could register was that her gut was telling her she desperately wanted to follow Conor into the woods.

But as if on cue, her common sense grew suddenly dominant: was she actually considering venturing in there right now? In her frazzled, vulnerable state? At night? In pursuit of answers she didn't even know the questions to? Trusting a foreign-sounding stranger to lead the way? For all she knew, Conor was a rapist or murderer. Or both. He'd admitted to spying on her. And though he looked too scrawny to physically overpower her (he didn't even appear much taller than she), Uncle Dale was also scrawny, and he had been able to effortlessly hold Eilwen against her will only just that afternoon. Men were always stronger than they looked.

Especially young ones.

Leaves and branches rustled and snapped. Conor was trying to hold branches apart for Eilwen's entrance. "Come on," he reminded innocently.

Eilwen stood, picking up Gracie. She took one step forward, then paused. "Are you sure?"

Conor looked at her almost pityingly.

"Eilwen," he said, and Eilwen was stunned at how effortlessly and perfectly he'd pronounced her name. No guessing his way through; no stuttering; no insulting, questioning tone. He'd simply said it. Acceptingly. He stepped back out of the trees. "There's no magic in the world that can make a person trust another. I could bewitch you if I knew how. You know, make you follow me against your will, or trick you into thinking you trusted me. But real trust is a magic that only familiarity can conjure. I want you to trust me, Eilwen. For your own sake. And I know you want to trust me, too."

Eilwen stiffened, wondering how he knew that.

"And I want you to come with me because it's what *you* want. And I want you to feel safe about it. So let's familiarize ourselves with each other." Conor cleared his throat. Eilwen cracked a smile at the comical seriousness he displayed in doing so. "I've already told ya my name – that's a sign of trust right there. *Never* give away your name to someone you don't trust yet. Remember that. Well, let's see, I hail from County Clare, Ireland – or at least, my mother does. I myself was born here, in these Kentucky woods. My magic's Fire, my sign's the Lion – just turned fourteen July twenty-eighth, I did. I speak five languages but only two fluently. And like nearly everyone else in the magical community, my Familiar's a cat. Her name's Molly. I'll introduce ya, if she'll finish cleaning and hop down from that tree already." Conor craned his neck toward a small poplar behind him.

Eilwen stared in bewilderment. "Did you say *magical community*?"

"I did." Conor leaned into the trees and, Eilwen was tickled to hear, meowed. She heard a faint but authentically feline "*Maow!*" respond.

"She'll be a moment," Conor informed. "She's just washed her paws. Doesn't want to dirty them again. She's

101

tiny still. Short legs. That's another reason I'd love you to come with me. Your snake being grown and all. You need to meet my mother. She'll be able to give you all the answers you need and more."

"Answers? About Gracie?"

"Aye. Mighty peculiar your Familiar's already matured. What age have you?"

"Thirteen."

"What's the day of your birth?"

"February twelfth," Eilwen said quietly. Mona had taught her to be ashamed of the fact that she shared a birthday with "that slimy slave-loving president."

Conor was halfway through a nod when he froze. "February?"

"Yes."

Conor shook his head. "That's wrong," he said simply, turning back to the trees.

"Wrong?"

"You were born this time of year. If you'd said October, or even June, it'd make more sense, but February's right out. Far too off the mark. Opposite sides of the year, even."

Eilwen stuttered, "I don't... understand."

"You will," said Conor reassuringly. "Am I glad I found you. And glad you found that clover. I never would've revealed myself of my own will." Eilwen thought she saw him blush.

Suddenly the bracken rustled and an orange tabby kitten emerged. Its ears were large for its head, as all kittens' were, and its body was slim – too old to still be nursing but not yet large enough to be a full-grown cat. All four paws were dipped in white and its eyes were fiery orange. As it bounded to Conor, Eilwen noticed strange bull's-eye shaped stripes on its sides.

What she noticed next was even more remarkable: the cat leapt into Conor's arms and shared with him a loving, intimate look Eilwen had only seen one place else.

"She's your Gracie."

"She's not," said Conor. "She's my Molly."

Eilwen could hear Molly purring. The cat looked stupidly content: eyes shut, furry mouth smiling, paws kneading the fabric of Conor's shirt. It was while studying the paws that Eilwen noticed how large they seemed for the cat's size. It was as though she were wearing mittens – furry white mittens one size too big.

Or as if she possessed extra digits.

"*Thumbs*," Eilwen gasped.

Gracie looked up, tongue flicking.

"Something the matter?" Conor asked. "Oh, how rude of me, you can pet her. Here…" He leapt over and held Molly out for Eilwen to touch.

Eilwen came to just enough to lift her hand and stroke the cat's cheek. After a moment, she managed, "How old is Molly?"

"Well, the same age as I have," said Conor with another warm smile, watching Eilwen pet the cat. "Isn't that the point of a Familiar, then? Or the reason they exist."

"Familiar?"

"An animal born the exact same time as you, right down to the second. Or in your case, hatched."

"I didn't hatch."

"But your Gracie did. You both drew your first breaths together, though you may have been miles apart at the time. It's the breath that connects you. Especially with your kind."

"What do you mean my *kind?*"

Conor pressed his lips. "In order to tell you that, I'll need to tell you something else."

"Something you need me to go into the woods for," Eilwen finished.

Conor gave a playfully over-innocent shrug.

Eilwen asked, "How old are you?"

"Fourteen. As I said before."

"*Maow!*" agreed Molly.

"Loud little thing," Eilwen observed. "So that means… what you're saying is… this cat… is fourteen years old."

"It does."

"And yet she's the size of a half-grown kitten."

"Well, I'm not the size of a full-grown man yet, am I? That's why you confound me, Miss Eilwen. Your lovely snake here," he inclined his head toward Gracie, who was posed like serpentine royalty by Eilwen's ear, "ought still be small. At the very least still have her hatchling's markings. But she's solid black. Adult-colored. And you're but twelve years of age!"

"I said I was thirteen." Eilwen was growing nervous. What did Gracie's adulthood entail? That Eilwen, too, would age early? Die an early death?

"Beggin' your pardon, but that can't be," Conor insisted respectfully. "Unless there's something off about both you *and* your snake. *Please* come see Mother. I'm scared for you. Truly. I've been watching you since your snake came to find you, and I've noticed several oddities that warrant concern. *Several.*"

"Why doesn't your mother come see me?"

"Because she... doesn't know about you." Conor sounded guilty.

Silence ensued. Eilwen didn't know how to fill it, nor did she want to, but Conor finally said, "I know how appalling this all sounds, but there's good to come of it. Good *has* come of it. I got your horse put away all right."

"That was you?"

"It wasn't *Dristan*," Conor spat.

"How did you do it?"

"I'm good with animals. And I used a calming spell."

"What are you that you can use spells and magic like that?"

"See, I really think you should be talking to Mother about all this."

Eilwen rubbed her head, heart racing. "That cat," she said, pointing at Molly. "You said she was fourteen years old. That she was alive fourteen years ago. Where did you find her?"

"I didn't. She found me."

"But where?"

"In this forest."

"Do you know where she came from?"

Conor looked puzzled. "An older, female cat –"

"*No*, damn it." Eilwen's eyes and throat burned. She struggled to find her voice again. "Do you know where she lived *before* she found you?"

"Oh, I do!" Conor realized. "Your farm, here. One of the men who lived here followed her the night she found me, as a matter of fact."

Eilwen's eyes flooded. "What did he look like?"

"Old. And heavy, I suppose. I was three, mind you, so anyone seemed large to me. He was chasing Molly with his life though."

Eilwen cupped her mouth and fell to the ground, sobbing. She didn't know what about, but it was far more powerful than anything that had set her bawling earlier. This touched her deeper. Went back further.

She honestly did not know if she were miserable or overjoyed.

Conor knelt beside her, dropping Molly. "I'm sorry," he said, panicked with concern. "I meant to say, young and thin."

He patted her back, but Eilwen gasped and flinched away. Conor withdrew his hand, looking lost.

"It was real," Eilwen sobbed. The realization that the fairytale that had kept her alive and sane these four lonely years... was *real*. It was too much. She didn't know if she was thrilled at discovering this tiny, sacred piece of him still living... or miserable that the familiarity of it felt like losing him all over again.

"What was real?" Conor's voice was soft. "You're not wondering if you're dreaming still, are you?"

Eilwen shook her head, wiping her eyes on her sleeve and wondering how in the world Conor had known she'd been worried about that. "For the first time," her voice shook, "I hope I'm not."

Conor looked desperately like he wanted to comfort her. But he did nothing for some time, sitting in silence while Eilwen cried into her coat. Finally, he leaned toward her ear. "Eilwen," he said gently. "I'm going to touch you now, all right?"

Eilwen, face buried, nodded. Conor reached down and slid a hand against hers, gauging her reaction. She flinched only slightly, but when she calmed again, he continued slowly until he had her entire hand in his.

"Come on," he said, tugging only gently. He used his other hand to help pull Eilwen to her feet. "I'll make it better. I promise."

* * *

Conor carried a flame in the palm of his hand to light the way.

With his other he held Eilwen's hand, leading her through the trees. Eventually they came upon a narrow, hardly visible footpath winding between the crowded trunks, and they walked it for some time, climbing over fallen logs, tiptoeing over brooks and creeks. Conor explained it was an old Indian game trail.

"I go hunting on this trail a lot," he said at one point. He tried several other times in a similar fashion to make conversation as they walked, but each time, Eilwen – still recovering emotionally, but also fascinated and in awe of the flame floating magically above his eternally outstretched palm – gave brief, distracted responses, and Conor would smile understandingly and simply try again a few minutes later.

When conversation finally began to flow, it was Eilwen who initiated: "You're the red-haired demon my granduncle saw."

"Demon?" Conor repeated dramatically, pretending to be hurt but smiling devilishly. Two pinpricks of light showed the fire reflected in his eyes. "That's hardly polite."

"You did steal his kitten."

"She was never his kitten," he snapped stubbornly. "She was always mine. And I always hers. We even found each other earlier than most."

"When do most find each other?"

"Right before they reach their thirteenth year. That's the magic birthday." Conor looked back at Eilwen just as she was reaching up to stroke Gracie, who rode on her shoulder. "That's why you can't yet be thirteen. A Familiar *always* finds her person before their thirteenth birthday. Doesn't matter how far apart they are. If you're already thirteen and she's still not found you, she likely never will."

"Are all Familiars 'she's?"

"No, but there are more 'she's than 'he's in the world. And 'she's are always more likely to be born magic."

"Magic…" Eilwen echoed the word. "It feels strange to say it out loud."

"There's a power to it, for sure. In fact, that's half of what magic is: thinking something, and then deciding to make it real with words."

"What's the other half?"

"Well, maybe that's a third of what magic is. And the other two thirds are…" He mumbled, counting on his fingers, then shook his head. "I'll just let Mother explain."

"And she'll definitely know what to do about my snake being grown?" Eilwen watched Molly trot speedily alongside Conor, scruffy kitten-tail held high.

"And if she doesn't," said Conor, "she'll know how to begin finding out."

"How far back do these woods go?" Eilwen asked after they had been on the game trail for what she felt was a disturbingly long amount of time. Hal's words echoed in her mind from what felt like an eternity ago: *It occurred to me that there shouldn't be so many trees — the woods shouldn't go this far.* What kind of illusion kept these intimate parts of the forest so well hidden? That demons and kittens could disappear and reappear as wanted, without any of the surrounding farming families ever glimpsing them?

"A fair bit." Conor tightened his grip on Eilwen's hand reassuringly. "It's safe. I swear to ya."

"Are you and your mother the only ones who live in here?"

"There are others." Conor paused. "Mother and I live on the fringes. Nearer the Border than the others."

"Border?"

"Magic spells that conceal our community from the mundanes."

"And a mundane is what I am," said Eilwen, to be sure she understood.

But Conor shook his head. "There's not a thing mundane about you. The folks who raised ya, though. They're mundanes."

Eilwen was puzzled and relieved all at once. Aunt Mona and Uncle Dale... perhaps even Gus, to an extent... she could easily see them all in a category separate from her own (though she had yet to even learn what her own category was). Old Hal, though. He hadn't been mundane, had he?

He couldn't have been.

"What about Dristan?" she asked.

Conor snorted. "What about him?"

"He isn't a mundane, is he?"

"Never met him, can't be sure. But anyway, it's because of the mundanes' encroachment that we've had to strengthen the Border over time. Especially during that alcohol-is-evil period they enacted a few years back. These trees used to be crawling with moonshiners. They still show up from time to time, but most get scared off."

"By what?"

"Oh, a whole number of things wanting to keep their forest secret. Sprites, goblins, dryads... The animals themselves work to fend off mundanes when they see them. There used to be more creatures in the wilderness here, back when Kentucky was so covered in trees that a squirrel could make it from Appalachia to the Mississippi without ever touching the ground. That was why the Native magic folk first created this secret coven – they wanted to preserve what they could, while they could."

"Indians live back here?" Eilwen asked, as an owl hooted overhead.

"Of course they do. The magic ones, at least. This community is theirs, after all. They just allow folks like

Mother and me to live with them. They call it *Igohida*. It means *Eternity*."

"So I'm walking into Eternity right now?"

Conor chuckled, "The rest of the magical world simply calls us the Bardstown Coven, if that's easier. Some still call it New Salem. It's whatever you prefer." He released Eilwen's hand to climb over a fallen tree that lay in their path, then reached back to help Eilwen, but paused immediately before making contact with her. "Forgot about your touching thing. I'm going to touch you now, Eilwen, all right?" He waited for Eilwen to look him in the eye and nod, then proceeded take her hand slowly and hold it steady while she clambered over the trunk and branches.

"You said there were magical animals," Eilwen said, lovingly stroking Gracie as they continued on the trail. "Goblins and sprites. Are there unicorns and dragons and mermaids too? What else is real?"

"Well, many are gone these days, I'm afraid. Unicorns aren't native to the Americas. And the native dragons died out centuries before the Cherokee witches created this place." He added optimistically, "I have seen a mermaid or two in the rivers round here. Tons of naiads as well. Could've sworn I saw an underwater panther once, but Ayasta – my best friend – told me it couldn't have been. Said they only live up in the Great Lakes. I like to tell myself it was an Uktena I saw in the water, and that maybe they're still alive and just hiding from us, the way we hide from the mundanes."

"Uktena?"

"One of the native dragons. The greatest of the North American dragons. Been extinct for over half a millennium. The Native mundanes were afraid of them and killed them all off, just as how the British mundanes killed all their own native dragons."

"That's terrible!" Eilwen pressed Gracie's head against her cheek; Gracie snuggled it affectionately.

"Aye, it's the misunderstood who always get the short end of things, isn't it? There are still European dragons, of course, but mostly in the German states and down near the Mediterranean. And none ever get very big anymore."

The trees increased in size and in distance from one another the further Eilwen and Conor walked. The game trail gradually opened into a widened footpath that disappeared altogether the further into the massive trees it stretched, for after a certain point no path was needed. Oaks, sycamores and pines towered higher than Eilwen's tired eyes could appreciate; their trunks, gnarled and mossy and draped with ferns, were like sparkling sylvan columns upholding a leafy canopy. Their lowest branches were well over fifty feet above Eilwen's head, and beams of silvery light, which could have only been from the moon, fell silently to the forest floor.

Eilwen took Gracie from her shoulder, deciding to carry her in her arms. There was an ethereal peacefulness in this part of the forest. Sparkling flecks of pollen floated through the air. Molly leapt after them. With both a soaring spirit and sinking heart, Eilwen realized this must be the place where Hal must have realized, once and for all, that he'd truly lost his kitten. This was the place where Hal had seen a toddling Conor and presumed him a fairy.

She could see why. There was an undeniable Fae-like quality to Conor as he lazily followed Molly, watching her bat at pollen with her mitten-like paws. His skin possessed a moonlike glow. His fiery hair caught a moonbeam and seemed to flair like the flame in his hand each time he and Molly spun around or changed direction. "Just a moment," he said. "She's almost done."

When Molly grew bored with the flecks, Conor put out the flame in his hand, scooped her up and cradled her. Then he, Molly, Eilwen and Gracie moved onward.

The trees crowded together, and Eilwen thought she saw an opening ahead. Conor walked faster, nearly skipping. Molly *maow*-ed in protest, leaping from his arms.

They stepped out of the trees and into a glade, in the center of which sat a little yellow cottage. The windows, which had diamond-shaped panes and forest-green shutters, glowed from the inside, making the vast floral gardens outside appear even darker. Off to the cottage's side was a barn, a few patches of fenced-off land with grazing cows and horses, and a vegetable garden. Eilwen gaped, absorbing the scene that seemed to have fallen directly out of a storybook.

"You live here?" she asked breathlessly. To think, this was back here in the forest she'd gazed at all her life.

"I do," said Conor. He made toward a winding path through the jungle of flowers that led to the cottage's green front door. "And you're welcome to too, if you'd like. It'd be better for you here. And safer. You're vulnerable to all sorts of nastiness at the moment. And I don't mean your aunt."

He held out his hand to her.

The ominousness and enticing vagueness of his words had both a fearful and exciting effect. And Eilwen Tabb, her magical snake in hand, once more followed the mysterious stranger who had appeared in the trees to whisk a lonely tobacco farmer away into the woods.

Chapter VI

Methodist Guilt

Sore tried and pained, the poor girl kept
Her faith, and trusted that her way,
So dark, would somewhere meet the day.
– John Greenleaf Whittier, "The Witch's Daughter"

"You should stay out here," Conor said, stepping from the path onto a small porch. He paused at the front door and held his chin. "Just for a minute. Until I explain everything." He glanced suspiciously at the door, as though it would spring to life and attack.

"Will I be safe out here?" asked Eilwen.

"Safer than I will be." Conor squared his shoulders and faced the door, looking like he was about to swing it open and stride inside, then sighed at the ground, hands on his hips. Then he took a deep breath, opened it, and tiptoed in, pulling the door to but not latching it. *"A Mháthair, tá mé sa bhaile."*

Eilwen blinked. Conor suddenly sounded like he was speaking gibberish.

"Agus cá raibh tú?" replied a voice from further inside.

It was a woman's. And though Eilwen had no inkling of what was being said, she knew and feared that tone of voice better than anything in the world. It was a tone on the verge of anger, like an agitated animal that would attack after just one more prod. It was Mona's every-day tone.

115

"*Bhí mé níláit,*" Conor was saying. "*Bhuel, bhí mé áit éigin. Ag feirm. Ag feirme thobac, a Mhaime.*"

"*An raibh tú, anois?*"

"*Bhí mé cinnte, ach…*"

Though Eilwen understood nothing of the exchange, she was uncomfortable eavesdropping, especially with the woman inside sounding so recognizably brusque. Placing her clover beneath Hal's cap, she took her moment alone with Gracie to study the garden and try to forget the fact that yet again her presence was likely angering someone. The strip of light from the door allowed her to identify some of the plants: lilies, foxgloves, bluebells, sunflowers, shrubs of viburnum, holly and forsythia, all draped in a raggedy quilt of trumpet vines tangled with morning glories. Only half the potential buds were in bloom. And the dark made all the leaves the same shade of green. But it was beautiful all the same. Lightning bugs waltzed all around.

Voices rose in the house. Conor, babbling away in whatever language he spoke, sounded defeated but persistent. "*Ach ní mór duit fheiceáil di. Labhair le di. Tá a fhios agam tá mé i dtrioblóid, ach tá sí anseo, mar sin labhairt léi.*"

"*A Chonor, beidh tú mo bháis. Lig sí taobh istigh.*"

The door creaked open.

Eilwen straightened. A tall woman stood in the doorway, looking down at her.

The woman appeared calculating, worn and wise, and yet somehow also so much resembled Conor in the face that Eilwen's nerves eased ever so slightly. The woman's white skin was only faintly wrinkled around her eyes, and her long, deep red hair was pinned in thick braids to the base of her neck. Her rusty-brown eyes – identical to Conor's – were sharply penetrating, but softened after only seconds of flitting imperceptibly over Eilwen's person. Nonetheless, Eilwen had instinctively prepared herself to be smacked, or worse, and flinched when the woman finally spoke. "Are you the tobacco farmer?"

Though her eyes were pitying, her tone sounded every bit as dangerous as it had speaking that other language. Eilwen piped, "Yes, ma'am."

The woman's studying of Eilwen intensified, though it almost appeared as though she were staring at something *around* Eilwen, instead of at Eilwen herself. "Has my son revealed himself to you at any time before tonight?" She, too, possessed an accent, far stronger than Conor's.

Eilwen shook her head. "No, ma'am."

The woman leered. "Come inside, then." She stepped aside, opening the door further, and muttered something angrily to Conor, who Eilwen saw stiffen obediently. The woman rolled her eyes at him. "Come inside, now, dear," she said suddenly very warmly to Eilwen. "'Tis not you I'm angry at. I beg you not be frightened. And after all, 'tis not your fault my son's an infuriating no-rule-abiding gremlin the likes of which –"

"Oh, indeed, always my fault," Conor sassed, but one look from his mother silenced him.

Eilwen hung her coat on a peg by the door. The first thing she noticed about the inside of the cottage was the warmth, and at no surprise: a strong fire blazed in a massive stone hearth, remarkably steadily and with no sign it would spark. The second thing she noticed was the airy openness, despite how small the cottage appeared from the outside. No obtrusive walls divided the rooms, but it was merely implied that one room ended and another began by the arrangement of the furnishings. There was a loft above a kitchen-like area, both of which took up the entire left half of the house, while the right half was devoted to writing and reading nooks, chests of stones and feathers and pieces of tree branches, cushioned sitting areas, and stacks and piles and shelves of books upon books: ancient-looking tomes with spines bearing titles in foreign languages, sometimes in foreign alphabets.

Eilwen had half a mind to pinch herself, but then remembered that if this *was* a dream, she didn't want to wake up.

Conor's mother asked Eilwen to take a seat by the fire. She then took a seat adjacent her, but stared at the fire for some time, looking pensive. Eilwen stroked Gracie, growing nervous.

Suddenly Conor's mother locked eyes on Eilwen. "How much do you know?" she demanded, clearly wanting to be direct but trying to keep from sounding intimidating. She failed; her eyes alone were more intimidating than Mona's entire bodily demeanor. If Mona glared daggers, this woman casually gazed swords. Eilwen felt as though this woman's rusty-brown stare could cut right through her.

Eilwen didn't know how to answer. She hadn't known when Conor had asked her either. "I know Gracie is… a Familiar. That's about it. And that there's a Border in the forest."

"The Border encompasses a hidden area in this forest of about thirteen square miles. That's nearly twice the size of Bardstown." Conor's mother crossed her legs. Her clothes were every bit as unusual as her son's – old-timey looking: an elaborately stitched dress-like tunic over a loose undershirt with the sleeves rolled up, and beneath the dress, which draped down no further than her knees, pants and very mud-stained leather boots. She smelled of rich, wet soil and pinesap, encompassed by the aroma of what Eilwen thought was cedar. "What's your name, child?"

"Eilwen Tabb."

Conor's mother's eyes widened infinitesimally. "What's your age?"

"I thought I was thirteen, but Conor said –"

"No, he's right, you can't yet be thirteen. Were you adopted? Is there any chance someone could have gotten your age mixed up with another child's? Or lied about it?"

"I was adopted, ma'am. Sort of. But I went straight from my mother to my aunt. So'd my brother."

"Maybe she *is* thirteen," mused Conor, popping up from behind his mother's chair. "Her snake's already grown. I'd wager the flukes are related."

"Possibly." Conor's mother kept staring at Eilwen. "You're clearly in a spot, here, aren't you?"

"I wouldn't know what I'm in, ma'am."

Conor's mother smiled faintly. "So my idiot son took it upon himself to explain Familiars, but didn't think to explain anything else along the way?" She stood and moved toward the kitchen.

"I didn't want to risk giving bad explanations!" said Conor.

"You've done enough talking tonight. Upstairs, now. Ready for bed. When you're finished you'll be making a bed for Eilwen, so hurry."

Conor slumped toward a ladder in the corner, disappearing into the loft above the kitchen. Molly *maow*-ed after him and hopped up the ladder step-by-step.

"You'll forgive him, as well," Conor's mother said while she moved about the kitchen. "He's a grouch by nature, and the time of day doesn't help."

"I can hear you!" snapped Conor's disembodied voice.

"*Hush!* He'll be good as gold when the sun's up. My name is Ygraine Sheehan." Conor's mother returned to her seat near Eilwen with a steaming mug in hand. "Call me Ygraine. Or you may call me ma'am, if ya wish. That's a hard habit to break, I'm sure."

"It is, ma'am." Curious and excited, Eilwen's uncertainty abated long enough for her to stammer happily, "Did you say *Sheehan*?"

"I did."

"That was my mother's name. Before marriage. She and my aunt were Sheehans."

"Were they?" Ygraine looked amused. "That makes you one of us. Maybe it was meant to be my Conor found you. You have a terribly Welsh first name. Tell me, who was your father?"

"Tom Tabb," Eilwen mumbled. "A fiendish drunk with no sense of responsibility."

"Sounds Irish enough." Ygraine handed Eilwen the mug. "You're mighty stressed. This'll calm you. Are you hungry at all?"

"Starving, ma'am."

120

"Good. I've got Conor's supper still waiting for him that he never touched. You can eat it."

"And what am I gonna eat?" Conor called.

"Gwydion Conor!" Ygraine practically roared. "This girl is your guest!"

"All I did was ask what I was gonna eat!"

"Then fix yourself something, for Goddess' bloody sake! Don't you have two working hands?" Conor groaned and Ygraine rolled her eyes again. Eilwen felt rude for having to hold back a giggle.

Ygraine's eyes settled calmly on Eilwen. "May I see your snake, dear?" She held out a hand that, though not disfigured, was covered in scars. Eilwen pulled her eyes from the faded marks, wondering at their history, then bundled Gracie's long black body and draped the coils on Ygraine's fingers. Gracie had gone still, not even daring to flick her tongue. She kept her yellow eyes fixed on Eilwen no matter which way Ygraine turned her.

Ygraine looked in awe of the black racer. "She's beautiful," she said fondly, and Eilwen thought she sounded almost surprised about something. "Snakes as Familiars are rare. And usually only belong to powerful individuals." She slid a careful finger along the ridge of Gracie's back, admiring her onyx scales, then handed her back to Eilwen. "You have potential, Eilwen. That much is clear at this point."

"Nothing else is clear?" Eilwen asked, the compliment flying right over her head.

"A few things. Your Element, for example, is plain as the nose on your face. Plain as your eyes, I should say. You're an Air witch."

Eilwen smiled to herself, pleasantly exhilarated at hearing herself verbally linked with the concept of air in such an important, official-sounding way. Though Eilwen barely understood what Ygraine meant by the wording of it, overall Eilwen could feel it made sense. It felt right. She had always enjoyed the breeze. Always felt there was magic, quite literally, in the air at times.

Then the word Ygraine had spoken after the word "air" registered and Eilwen thought she would be sick to her stomach. "Did you say *witch*?"

Ygraine closed her eyes and nodded, as though in expectance of such a reaction. She said, with the air of one imparting somber news but being secretly thrilled about it, "I did."

Eilwen stared in silence.

"...Are you sure that's what you said?"

"Fairly sure, dear."

"I – how do you know? What do you mean by *witch*?" Words were funny things after all, weren't they? What one word meant to one person meant something different to another. A lightning bug in Kentucky was a firefly to a Hoosier. A violin in another city was a fiddle here in Bardstown. A Democrat to Louisville was a lazy low-lifed liberal to the rest of the state. That was all this was, wasn't it? Some unfortunate colloquial mix-up?

But even if it was... it would still all mean the same thing.

Witch.

Eilwen began breathing fast, running her fingers through her hair, dislodging Hal's cap. She suddenly remembered Conor's comment in the forest about

Cherokee witches, and wondered why it hadn't bothered her.

"But are you really surprised? Come now, think on it a bit."

Eilwen did think on it. She thought she couldn't stop. A witch. She couldn't be. Fairies and magic were one thing, their own thing entirely. But *witches*... They were evil. They were the stuff of nightmares and frightening children's tales. One of Eilwen's own neighbors, Miss Beulah, was an old widowed woman whom local children liked to say was a witch. They told of her throwing naughty children to the giant snapping turtle that dwelled in her pond. They even told of her seeing the future, and mixing potions of cat's blood and crow's feathers. If Eilwen was a witch, she would never be allowed in church again. Her minister would have her lynched. And Mona would set up picnic to watch.

Not that Eilwen was aghast at there being something magical about her. Hal himself had believed so. And Eilwen had always known she'd been different. Magic had been an acceptable – and favorite – explanation. Comforting, no matter how farfetched. She had even convinced herself she was a Changeling once when she was eleven. But *witch* had never crossed her mind, not even in jest. Witches worshipped the Devil and ate children. They conjured demons, and cackled as they flew through the night on broomsticks. Despite Mona's insistence otherwise, Eilwen had always believed that God would welcome her into Heaven when she died. Love her the way His son had loved the children in the Bible. That He would end her suffering. That Heaven would make it all worth it. And though she disagreed with God's stance on snakes, she had prayed desperately to Him every Sunday for years to tell Hal for her that she couldn't wait to see him again. What would all that mean, then, if she was a witch? Was all that praying wasted?

Had it been useless to begin with?

What if being a witch *was* the magical explanation for everything? What if this frighteningly plausible possibility explained the fondness she'd always possessed for serpent-kind? Eilwen looked down at Gracie, snuggled in her lap beneath Hal's cap, and for the first time in her life did not see an innocent and misunderstood victim of social bias. Did not see the loving loyal friend that had given her hope and purpose the past few days. She saw only the shadow of the serpent that had tempted Eve.

But Gracie, as though sensing Eilwen's sudden ire, lifted her head and pulled away from her, and Eilwen's heart lurched with such hurt that she whimpered. Confusion overwhelmed her. Guilt ate at her as she tried to coax Gracie back toward her, then took her in her arms and held her as tightly as she'd once held the doll of the same name. How could she have ever equated this beautiful animal to evil? Gracie was the single most precious thing in her life right now. But then guilt for siding with the snake hit her, and Eilwen buried her face in Gracie's coils, feeling even more lost than she had while weeping under the oak tree.

Part of her wasn't sure she wasn't still doing something evil. She'd been told all her life she was evil, after all. And the Devil was crafty. Was it possible Eilwen's inexplicable love for Gracie was a trick? The work of demons? Old

Hal had called Conor a devil. Had he been right in doing so?

"You are a mess, aren't you?" Ygraine's voice was jarringly tender. Eilwen, face still buried in Gracie's coils, heard Ygraine stand and return to the kitchen. "I'll get Conor's supper for ya. You need to eat. And here I thought Catholics were the masters of guilt. What are ya, dear, Lutheran?"

Eilwen raised her head slightly, staring into the black void Gracie's coils created. "Methodist."

Ygraine made a *Tuh!* sound. "What are ya doing farming tobacco, then?"

"It makes money," said Eilwen, confused at the question. "More than twice our corn and barley make together."

"Yet are not Methodists forbidden to pollute the human form with alcohol or smoking?" When Eilwen didn't answer, Ygraine continued, "You don't find it a bit contradictory, ignorin' God's will to farm what you believe to be a bodily poison just to make a profit?"

"Well… it's not all for smoking. People chew it."

"Yet still more smoke it."

Eilwen lifted her head further.

"Drink the mug I gave ya," Ygraine ordered, returning with a plateful of stew that smelled like deer meat. Eilwen raised the mug in her hand and stared distrustingly at it. Ygraine snapped, "It won't turn ya into a rat."

"What will it turn me into?" Eilwen asked without thinking.

"Drink, Eilwen." Ygraine's sharpness sounded more maternal than threatening.

Eilwen brought the mug to her lips and drank, and was (pleasantly) surprised to discover that within minutes of swallowing only one mouthful of the comfortably hot liquid, she felt a weight lift from her chest she had not even been aware had been pressing on her. It was as if it had always been there – she had simply grown used to it. And its sudden absence confused and relaxed. Gracie lifted her head and examined the contents of the mug. Eilwen smiled at the snake as she flicked her tongue over the drink, then flicked her tongue ticklingly against Eilwen's nose.

Then Conor descended the ladder in the corner and Gracie hissed disapprovingly.

"What?" Conor demanded of Gracie as he hopped the back of the sofa-like seat on which Eilwen rested, holding a pile of blankets and quilts. He landed bouncingly beside Eilwen and smiled. "Up with ya. We need to make your bed for the night."

Eilwen helped Conor spread blankets upon the sofa and tuck warm quilts all about its cushions, then the two of them sat together on the makeshift bed, Eilwen hungrily devouring the plate of stew Ygraine had given her while Conor peeled an apple with a small knife made of bone. The fire crackled as they ate. Gracie eventually lowered her guard and ceased staring at Conor long enough to curl up in Eilwen's lap and fall asleep.

"She doesn't seem to like you," Eilwen blurted observantly before she could stop herself.

"I imagine Conor's been harassing the little beastie for some time." Ygraine joined them in the sitting area.

"Harassing?" Eilwen asked.

Conor snorted.

"Not that I approve," Ygraine sighed, "but apparently Conor's been watching you a while. Ever since he noticed your snake in the woods. She must have come from far away indeed to find ya, dear, if her presence struck him as unusual. Conor spends much of his time in the forest near this part of the Border and he knows every squirrel and every knot in every tree."

Conor said nothing but straightened up proudly.

"Why don't we all go to bed? Certainly Eilwen's tired. She's had such an... *informative* day." Ygraine rose from her seat.

"But I'm not sleepy, I swear," Eilwen pleaded. She wanted to learn more – hunt for some silver lining of salvation in the damning knowledge that she was a witch. She didn't feel safe falling asleep with that discovery fresh on her mind. Should she even be able to relax enough to fall asleep, her nightmares alone would be excruciating.

But Ygraine glanced at her and smirked. "Eilwen, dear," she said, almost condescendingly, "I'll save you all kinds of future trouble and embarrassment by tellin' ya right now: it's of no use to lie to a Fire witch."

"Or warlock," said Conor.

"We're born able to detect when people lie as naturally as a bat is born able to see sound."

Eilwen's face grew flushed. "What'd I lie about?"

"Your aura flared when you said you weren't tired. You're exhausted. For your sake, dear, let yourself fall asleep. That tonic you drank should keep your nerves from botherin' ya." Ygraine made for the kitchen. "Conor, let her be, now."

127

Conor handed Eilwen half of his apple, having already eaten the other half. "Sweet dreams, Eilwen," he said. He paused awkwardly as though to add something, but instead disappeared up the ladder to his loft. Molly followed suit.

The fire dimmed. The cabin darkened, save for a few spots of candlelight in the kitchen. "I'll be finished in just a moment, Eilwen," Ygraine said, bent over a massive book on a wooden table. "Then I'll put out the lights and let you sleep."

Eilwen peered curiously at Ygraine's efforts. "What are you doing?"

"Pressing leaves, before they wilt too much to bother preserving."

Eilwen looped Gracie around her neck, then left the sofa and approached the table. She watched Ygraine smooth out what looked like a sunflower leaf, then asked, "Could you press something for me, please?"

"What have ya?"

Eilwen lifted Hal's cap and carefully pulled her clover out of her hair. She was disheartened by how much it had wilted, but Ygraine didn't look concerned. "That you had a clover on your person was the only reason I didn't wring Conor's neck tonight," she said, taking the clover and examining it.

"I found it right before I saw him. Can you save it?" said Eilwen. "It's my first one, I don't want to lose it."

"Of course I can save it." Ygraine placed the clover in the bottom corner of the page, arranging the leaves into the iconic four-leaf shape with the stem down the middle. She shut the book and tightened its several buckling clasps. "I'll finish the rest of my pressing in the morning. Go to sleep now, Eilwen."

Eilwen returned to her bed by the fire and unlaced her boots. She kept them and Hal's cap on the floor together, then snuggled up with Gracie beneath the quilts. The fire dimmed further, as though out of consideration; only embers pulsed in the darkness. Eilwen closed her tired eyes and prayed.

She prayed God would forgive her for being born out of wedlock. She prayed He would forgive her for being a witch, if this proved to be true. She prayed for Old Hal, in case – just in case – he, too, had been evil and not known it.

* * *

The house was quiet. Eilwen lay in the dark, sleepy but sleepless.

She should have known God didn't want bastards. He had probably handed her soul to Satan the moment she'd formed in her unwed mother's belly. Mona and the rest of the world were right: Eilwen had been a lost cause from the beginning.

Curiously, stroking Gracie did not feed these Hellish fears. It eased them. If Eilwen had been bolder, she would have thought God was trying to reach her through Gracie. Maybe even *love* her through Gracie. If Gracie were a tool of the Devil's, Eilwen should not feel so loved around her. The Devil couldn't mimic love.

Eilwen knew what love was. Hal had loved her. When Eilwen was with Gracie, she felt as she had when Hal used to pull her into his lap and rock. If she had been bolder, she would have wondered if Hal had not been something of a demon himself.

She wished she'd had greater presence of mind to question Ygraine further when she'd had the chance. Ygraine had made a practical argument – the kind that, no matter the level of ignorance, a human being's logical nature cannot resist entertaining. Why *did* the Hittles farm tobacco? Was it sinful to profit off the sins of others? Did the two sins cancel each other out?

She wished she could sleep, despite the threat of nightmares. But her mind was a motor that had been given a full tank of gas. There was nothing to do but let it run. She could at least close her eyes while she waited…

"Eilwen!" A voice from above hissed her name.

Eilwen sat up. She looked up to see Conor poking his head through the railing of his loft. Light from behind – silvery moonlight – gave his red hair an eerie halo.

"What?" she whispered back.

"Are you busy?"

"Busy?"

"Are you trying to sleep?"

"Yeah."

"Come up here."

Eilwen knit her brows. "Right now?"

Conor's head bobbed in a nod.

"Aren't you trying to sleep?" Eilwen asked.

"Of course I'm not. Climb the ladder." He pulled his head from the railing and disappeared.

Gracie was sound asleep, and as she disliked Conor anyway, Eilwen let her remain on the sofa, then tiptoed across the sitting area toward the ladder in the corner. She climbed quietly. When she reached the top, she faced a wide diamond-paned window looking into a starry sky and a horizon of black treetops. Stunned at the beauty, she didn't notice Conor beside her.

He reached for her, then stopped. "I'm going to touch you, again," he warned.

Eilwen jumped, but nodded. Conor gently took her wrist and helped her the rest of the way onto the loft. Eilwen, used to scaling greater and less stable heights in the curing barn, needed no assistance, but found she enjoyed Conor's soft, respectful touch.

Conor's loft had everything Eilwen would have loved in a bedroom of her own – including a bed. He had bookshelves bearing birds' nests, pinecones, jars of feathers and dried plants, and pieces of quartz and other crystals. There was a chest with clothes messily hanging out, and beside it, another chest holding books and scrolls. Above, on the walls that were not the massive window, were tattered maps, and ornaments of feathers, beads and animal furs. Books lay scattered and open in the middle of the floor, which bore a red braided rug. Amid the books, Molly lay stretching; she was purring, so her *maow* of greeting when she saw Eilwen sounded like a trill.

Eilwen stepped slowly, gazing around in admiration. Above her hung glittering mobiles shaped like stars and moons. Some were just crystals cut like jewels – when they caught the moonlight they burned and twinkled as though on fire.

"I don't like how little she told you." Conor sat down on the floor by Molly. Apparently he'd been awake a while. "I can tell how confused you are. You weren't sleeping."

Eilwen pulled her gaze from the mobiles down to Conor. "How could you tell?"

Conor patted the floor beside him, and Eilwen sat. "I'm a Fire. I can see your light. Your color's terribly confused right now."

"My… color?"

"Your aura. There, see? You're even more confused. I can see it darkening. It grows muddier the worse you get."

Eilwen stared.

Conor smiled and said, "Your electromagnetic field." He began flipping through one of his books. "Every living thing has one. We all sense them whether we know it or not, but only a few can *see* them. I'm one of those few," he added with a joking cockiness that made Eilwen chuckle. His smile widened.

"Because you're a Fire witch?" said Eilwen.

Conor's smile faded. "Fire *warlock*."

"Oh, sorry. And Ygra – your mother, said I was –"

"An Air witch." Conor seemed to have found the page he was looking for. "You can read about yourself. There's loads of information on Air witches. I supposed if you're gonna grow up not knowing what you are, it's best to be something so common."

He handed Eilwen the book, and she asked, feeling almost relieved, "I'm common?"

"Terribly so. And I don't mean that badly! But it's a simple fact is all. About half of all births are to Air."

Eilwen studied the page to which the book was opened. Columns of calligraphied text floated amid drawings of

132

swirling clouds and stylized wind currents. There was one drawing of a woman's face, bearing eyes of yellow, and Eilwen's heart skipped. Placed around the woman were drawings formed of tiny stars, which Conor explained were the constellations connected to the Element. "Aquarius, Gemini, and Libra." He finished by pointing at the star drawing that looked like a set of scales. "I think that's you, right there. Libra."

"Why's that?"

"You're about to turn thirteen, aren't you? And the sun's about to enter Libra. You have to be born to Air to be an Air."

Eilwen reverently touched the symbol of the scales. "How many types of witches are there?"

"Just the four. Air's the commonest, then Water, then Earth, and Fire's the rarest."

"You like that, don't you?" Eilwen grinned at him, and even in the darkness Eilwen could see Conor blush.

But he shrugged. "Rare's just a better word for lonely." He stroked Molly, who yawned and meowed. She couldn't do anything without meowing at someone, it seemed.

When a very meow-like sound reverberated from nowhere else but the large window behind them, Eilwen and Conor both jerked around. Eilwen experienced a jolt of panic: nothing but glass separated her from the daunting face of a moon-eyed cougar.

The big cat *mrowed*, then lifted a giant paw and batted at the pane. Eilwen gaped as Conor sighed in annoyance and scooted toward the window with the air of one grudgingly letting a whining barn cat into the house. "It's only Sheba," he said over his shoulder to Eilwen, having, in his irritation, only just realized how needlessly afraid she was. "Mother's Familiar. Or rather... Well, it's a long story. Point is, she won't hurt ya.

"You brute, why didn't ya go to Mother's window?" Conor opened part of the window and Sheba slipped silently inside. The mountain lion paused long enough to snort at him before padding in utter silence toward the ladder and leaping noiselessly to the floor below. "She's been out hunting and is spying on us. She'll tell Mother we were up this late and we'll hear about it in the morning." Conor shook his head disapprovingly, as though he were the parent and Ygraine the troublesome child.

"But anyway," he said, sitting beside Eilwen again. "Take that book. It might help ya sleep. Your color's already cleared a bit. Still muddy, though."

Eilwen closed the book and looked at Conor. "Thank you," she said. "For everything. I'd be shivering under that oak tree right now if you hadn't helped me."

"D'you expect me to leave a pretty thing like you crying by your lonesome?" Conor seemed to have only just realized what he said, for he blushed violently. Eilwen felt her own face grow hot and noticed Conor suddenly relax.

"You and your mother have been so kind," Eilwen said, feeling just as uncomfortably undeserving as she had the afternoon she'd spent at Lily Lane. What did it say about her that the only people in the world who had ever shown her kindness and understanding were Catholics and witches? "I don't deserve it."

Conor shook his head. "I'd say the opposite. You're overdue for kindness. You're long overdue for a lot of things."

* * *

When Eilwen awoke the following morning, there was something pinned to the sofa cushion near her head. Two things, in fact – a single yellow coneflower, and with it, a note:

I'm sorry I stole your granduncle's kitten.

Chapter VII

Shattered Misconceptions

Science advanced, in grandeur and reality, analyzing every thing,
This world all spann'd with iron rails...
– Walt Whitman, "Song of the Exposition"

Eilwen smiled at the note and flower to which she'd woken, pocketing the note and placing the flower behind her ear.

Memories of the previous night returned, brightened by the sweetness of Conor's gesture. Eilwen was happy none of it had been a dream. At long last, Eilwen Tabb had found her four-leaf clover, and discovered more than fairies: she'd discovered who she was. Or partially. But it was enough. It explained enough.

She was a witch.

The word still shocked her. But she was excited – that, she couldn't deny. Before she'd opened her eyes, she'd been frightened she would wake up in her dark cold room with straw stuck in her hair. Part of her had been convinced she'd dreamt up Conor, Ygraine and this elaborate magical explanation. And part of her still worried that she was relieved it wasn't a dream: it was wrong for her to want this to be real. To want to be a witch.

But Conor's book had made sense. She had read through as much as she could before her eyes had gone sore. It had offered reasons for everything Eilwen had always thought were faults on her part – things that, it turned out, were not faults but simple characteristics of her supposed "airy" nature. Her daydreaming, her sensitivity to smoke and smell and noise, her uncanny and eidetic hearing that rivaled even Shep's. Eilwen had always possessed good hearing. She remembered everything she heard and could replicate it with the accuracy of a recording in some instances; in the first grade, during her first ever music class, Eilwen had embarrassed Miss Ethel by insisting her sheet music was wrong and then demonstrating the fact by plucking out the proper notes on the piano. (Eilwen had never touched a musical instrument before that day and Mona had forbidden her to indulge in any formal musical endeavor since.) Apparently Eilwen was sensitive to sound not by weakness, but by nature. Sensitive to changes in the air and how it moved. If Eilwen was a witch – if this was, indeed, the truth about her – then she would be able to say that she had talent. *Talent*, and not a flaw.

Old Hal had said she had a better flair for air curing than any farmer he'd known. He'd admired and trusted her ability to identify what good soil smelled like.

Eilwen sat up on the couch. Had Hal known what she was?

And the Homestead. Was she to go on living there, with the knowledge that she belonged somewhere else? With others like her? Conor had said last night that it would be "safer" for her to remain with him and his mother. Said she was "vulnerable to all sorts of nastiness." What had he meant?

The house was silent as Eilwen slipped on her boots. Whether she remained here or not, she knew one thing: Dristan had to know.

She was relieved to find Conor and Ygraine in the garden. She would have felt rude leaving without telling them.

"But you can't leave!" Conor hopped down from the empty birdbath on which he'd been perched sharpening his bone knife. He turned to Ygraine. "Tell her why she can't leave!"

"She can leave, and I won't be stopping her if she feels she must," Ygraine replied with a note of regret. She stood from harvesting marigolds and approached Eilwen. "I trust you're smart enough to know to keep this place secret from the mundanes."

"But... just from mundanes, right?"

"So there's another one like you," Ygraine realized. "A friend you think is a witch as well?"

"His name is Dristan McAtee. He has an otter."

"And after you tell him what he is, you'll come back?" Conor said to Eilwen, eyes wide.

"Should I be worried?" Eilwen asked Ygraine. "Am I safe outside the Border?"

"You're always safer in the Border than out. And your magic's aroused, now that you've united with your Familiar, so you're far more sensitive than you've ever been before. Vulnerable to things that mightn't have affected you before."

"So I wasn't magical before I found Gracie?"

"Of course you were. But finding Gracie ignited a growth of it in ya. Magical puberty, one could say. Where does this Dristan boy live?"

"One farm over from me."

"Nearby, then. Conor, go with her. You know better than she what's dangerous to her right now."

Conor fixed Eilwen and himself a breakfast of eggs, bread, deer meat, and all sorts of fruits and vegetables. Before they left, he handed her an uncooked egg. "Your snake might be hungry."

Gracie was looped around Eilwen's shoulders. Eilwen offered her the egg. She nosed it first, then took it slowly, mouth widening and scaled black lips sliding around the brown shell. The skin connecting her jaw stretched, a quilt of gray scales; Eilwen and Conor watched, fascinated, as the egg gradually disappeared. Once the bulge passed Gracie's head, powerful throat muscles cracked and crushed. "Neat," Eilwen said. Conor smiled at her.

About a minute later, Gracie hacked nastily and expelled a slimy crushed eggshell onto Eilwen's shirt. Eilwen groaned and Conor burst out laughing.

"I swear, I didn't know she'd do that," Conor insisted, still laughing, as he and Eilwen walked through the forest back the way they'd come last night. "At least not on your shirt."

"Fine, okay," Eilwen chuckled, pretending not to believe him. When she smiled teasingly and glanced at him, he burst out laughing again. "Oh, that's not suspicious at all."

"It's funny, I can't help it!"

"Sure you can't. Hey, where's Molly?"

"Stayed behind. Hunting mice in the barn. Mother says it's healthy to practice being away from your Familiar sometimes."

"What was it you kept calling her last night? *Why-muh?*"

"*Mhaime*," said Conor. "It's the Irish for 'Mom.'"

"Is that the language you were speaking?"

"It was."

"Is that one of the two languages you're fluent in?"

"It is indeed. The other's English. I'm fairly confident I'm fairly fluent in the Latin, but my Welsh and Cornish leave a lot to be desired."

"You know any Scottish?"

"Don't be ridiculous."

The massive, ancient trees through which they trekked were what Conor referred to as "old growth," and he proceeded to explain, with an audible note of despair in his voice (Eilwen thought with a smile that Conor's voice betrayed his emotions every bit as easily as her aura must betray herself; it seemed to rise and fall, passionately and authentically, with whatever emotion he felt) that there was scarcely any old growth left these days, and that what little remained was rapidly disappearing.

"Can't we stop it?" Eilwen asked. "Save the old growth with magic?"

"We try and sometimes succeed, such as with New Salem here. But mundanes are fond of iron – one of the things to which you're becoming increasingly vulnerable. Magic doesn't make one all-powerful, as mundanes are wont to believe. It allows you to do things others can't, and that's an advantage in the right circumstances, but it's no fix-all, and even causes problems of its own. Iron has been magic's downfall for centuries, and it's damn near impossible to fight its advance."

"Why's iron bad?"

"Just bad for magic folk. Mundanes are mostly immune to it. It'll make folks like you and me frightful sick, though. Iron's immune to magic and impossible to detect by magic, so the only way to know if iron's near ya is to gauge how sick or weak you feel, but even then it might be something other than iron causing it. Just a moment, now. Come here, Eilwen, I, uh... I'll be needing to touch you again. For only a second."

Conor stopped walking and Eilwen inched toward him. Conor, uncharacteristically serious, lifted a hand and softly touched two fingers to her neck. He was silent, ignoring Gracie's hissing at him, then asked, "Can you feel that?"

"Feel what?" said Eilwen nervously. "What are you doing?"

Conor's expression brightened. "Nothing, then! We're all right." He continued down the path, beckoning her to follow.

Eilwen felt her neck, patting the spot he'd touched. "What was that about?"

"Testing to see you'd be safe out here."

"From what? Iron?"

"Well... other things besides. Iron hasn't a will of its own, and no magic person would utilize it for fear of the iron hurting their own selves, so you only need be fearing the metal where mundanes are concerned. They're the iron wielders. But other magic folk can hurt ya with magic, and as Mother said, you're freshly vulnerable. Magic's all around us all the time – energy that swirls about the earth like wind. Which is one of the reasons four-leaf clovers are good luck. As you learned last night, they let their finders see right through enchantments. But only surface enchantments," he added, stressing the importance. "Light magic. Deep magic's different. That was deep magic I tried on ya back there." He stopped and looked at her. "You did feel nothing, right? Nothing at all?"

Eilwen shook her head. "There's a connection, isn't there? Between my vulnerability level and me not feeling what you did."

"There's a connection. Damn. Mother had wanted to explain this…"

"Explain what?"

"So I don't know why she got angry last night, she clearly doesn't trust my explanations…" He finished ranting to himself. "You fainted when you first met Gracie, didn't ya?"

In her enthusiasm, Eilwen choked on her "Yes!" This was one of the things she'd wanted to ask Ygraine about. "My friend Dristan fainted around the time he found his otter, too!"

"Witches raised in mundane environments have that reaction. Finding your Familiar is what sets the magic in you growing. You weren't raised in a magical way, or maybe had been around too much iron growing up, so when Gracie set your magic growing you weren't used to the strength of it and fainted. It can be overwhelming."

"I also had a headache," Eilwen volunteered, as they splashed across the shallows of a creek, Conor taking comically calculated strides in order to avoid the water as much as possible. "Everything was too loud. It hurt to hear. Was that because... I read in your book Air witches are sensitive to sound?"

"The noise headache *is* popular with your type."

"What kind of ache do Fire witches get?"

Conor retorted, "I'm a warlock. And I wouldn't know. I was raised with magic."

They reached the other side of the creek, Conor stopping in frustration to shake off what little water clung to his boots. "It's sort of like..." He twirled his hands. "Like music, I suppose. You're Air, you'll appreciate this. If you've no ear for music, a sour note won't bother you, will it? But if you suddenly acquire a musical ear, bad notes bother you greatly – you even cringe at the sound of impure notes you might've once thought clean. Finding Gracie gave you your... ear... for magic. And now you're sensitive to it. Even the bad. That puts you in danger."

"I'm vulnerable to magical sour notes?" Eilwen teased.

"You know what I mean. But that's why I'm with ya. I'm more experienced and I'll be knowing what to do should you succumb to anything while we're out of the Border."

Eilwen was silent a while. "That means... That means you're definitely expecting me to go back, then."

"And why wouldn't ya?" Conor tried to sound casual, but Eilwen could hear the worry in his voice. "It's all too often that witches and warlocks born to mundanes go their whole lives never being allowed to be who they are. Never even knowing why they're different. Why they're suffering. Why they can't make themselves be like everyone else, no matter how hard they try."

Eilwen felt a lump in her throat.

"The coven leaders don't allow every person who displays an affinity for magic to join the coven. And the way Mother was acting, Eilwen... Well, it's seeming to me there's a chance you'll be allowed to join! To live with us. We'll take care of you, and teach you, and let you be who you are. Eilwen, if you so wanted, you might never have to lay sight on that wretched homestead of yours again after today."

* * *

Eilwen got down on hands and knees and peered under the hydrangea.

"Gus."

She sighed and scrambled as far into the branchy cave as her size allowed her anymore; she used to be able to fit all the way in — conceal herself completely within the leaves and bobbing snowball blossoms — but these days she could only fit into the natural nook as far up as her waist. Gus, however, was still small enough to hole himself away, as he had done. "Gus, I'm sorry."

He was curled up against the trunks, shuddering and wailing as though he'd been stuck by a knife. "No you're not!" His voice was muffled, turned away from Eilwen. His little body shook with each new sob.

"Yes, I am!" Eilwen insisted pleadingly. She glanced fearfully toward the porch, against which the subsequently one-sided hydrangea grew. "I'm sorry! I am! Don't cry, now!"

"You're not sorry!" Gus's chubby face was red; it glistened wet when he looked at her. "You only just want me to don't tell Aunt what you di-hi-iiid!" His breathing came in jolts and he turned away again, hugging the hydrangea.

144

Panic built in Eilwen's chest. Gus was right. And if he kept crying like this, Aunt would hear the racket and there'd be no need to tell on Eilwen anyway. "I'm sorry I hit you, Gus, I am!"

She reached out to touch him but Gus squealed and pulled away, scooting further into the leaves. "No! You're mean and I hate you and go away!" The wail he gave then sounded as though saying those words pained him more than the smack to the face Eilwen had given him only minutes ago.

Eilwen froze, her insides suddenly heavy.

She had hurt more than her little brother's cheek. She'd hurt his feelings. Gus wasn't crying because he'd been hit. He was crying because Eilwen had been the one who'd hit him.

Eilwen lowered herself onto her stomach, propped up by her elbows. Her legs stretched out behind her, sticking out of the bottom of the bush as though it had fallen on top of her. She guiltily fiddled with a pebble in the dusty dirt and looked at Gus. The steady sound of his weeping seemed at odds with the occasional chirping bird, and cheerfully dappled sunlight that touched him through the leaves.

"Does it hurt still?"

Gus wailed again. "Uh-huh."

He still wouldn't look at her.

Eilwen watched him in silence.

When he hadn't wailed in a while, she asked, "Can I kiss it and make it better?"

Gus pressed his palms to his eyes and wiped them. "Uh-huh."

He sniffled and crawled forward. Eilwen sat up as much as she could within the mouth of the hydrangea. Gus's face was still contorted with crying as he reached her and pushed into her lap, clinging to her, burying his face in her shirt as though she were the only other person in the entire world right now.

Eilwen stared at the hydrangea, hands in her pockets. Gracie hung from an oak branch behind her.

For the past four years, Eilwen had wanted nothing more than to be able to leave the Hittles. There had been nothing keeping her here after Hal had died. Nothing except the very basic and condemningly unavoidable fact that she had nowhere else to go.

But now she did.

Why, then, did she suddenly feel there *was* something keeping her here? More than merely the tobacco?

The memory of the day she had smacked a toddling Gus across the face in the fashion of every smack she'd ever received from Mona, and sent him crying beneath the sheltering bows of the hydrangea growing up against the side of the porch, clung to her. His cry of shock and pain after her hand had made contact with his cheek replayed in her mind like a recording. There were times when Eilwen was grateful for the fact that her ears were sentimental enough to store every sound that touched them. Every word uttered to her. Every note in every song she'd ever heard. And there were times such as this, when she wished to deafen herself, to escape ever hearing and thus eternally preserving anything horrible again.

Gus had asked her why she'd done it. Why she'd lashed out. Truthfully, Eilwen hadn't known. All she'd known was that she had been angry. Not at Gus – she hadn't known what she had been angry at. Eilwen had simply been sitting on the porch steps, deep in thought about the fact that she hadn't heard Hal's voice in six months, holding her knees to her chest to keep her feet from touching the back of his gravestone, and Gus, wandering

146

up to tell her Mona wanted her to kill a chicken for dinner, had simply been at the wrong place at the wrong time.

That first year had been the worst. That was the year Eilwen had fulfilled the predictions of every accusation of evil and wickedness ever thrown at her. Eilwen's tenth year of life had been one of anger, misery, and flaring tempers that had frightened even herself. Eilwen had not understood her behavior that year. She hadn't known what grieving was. And even had she known, she hadn't been allowed to grieve. Missing Hal was forbidden. Anger had been her outlet.

How odd that Eilwen's thirteenth year was promising to be her most glorious. If she could only allow herself to sever the ties she'd always wanted severed. But in her dreams of severing ties with the Hittles, it had always been just with the Hittles – never the Homestead. Never Gus. Never the farm or the crops.

Eilwen and Conor had been making their way across the fields toward Bloomfield Road when Eilwen had slowed her pace upon passing the farmhouse and meandered to a halt beneath the oak nearest the porch. The Ford pickup was nowhere to be seen, so Eilwen knew the Hittles and Gus were in town right now, sitting in church, and would not be home for hours. Silent and empty and peaceful, the Homestead had stirred within her a wave of nostalgia she had never imagined she would feel for the place.

She would miss it, she realized.

"Just a minute," she'd told Conor in response to his urging her onward. He'd nodded in understanding and gone to have a look around.

Eilwen turned from the hydrangea and stepped up against the side of the house, her back to the hewn poplar logs, then methodically stepped forward toward the middle of the grassy sideyard, heel-to-toe, counting each step. When she reached step thirty-five, she stopped.

"Hey, Hal."

She stared at the ground, hands in her pockets. With her right, she pulled out the note Conor had left her that morning. She knelt and dug a small hole in the earth, placing the note inside and covering it. The lump in her throat rose again and her eyes stung, but she was smiling. "He says he's sorry."

"On our way back to the Border we need to stop at the Homestead again," Eilwen said as she and Conor turned onto Lily Lane.

"Why?" he asked.

"There's something in my room I need to get before I leave. Also I want you to meet my brother, Gus, in case he's a witch –"

"*Warlock.*"

"– in case he's a warlock too."

The sky was cerulean and not a cloud was to be seen. The sun still crept upwards, having not yet risen above the trees, but its sharp first beams pierced the leaves. Thelma Duvall's goats bleated as they grazed, the grass in their small field blue and glittering.

"Anyone else?" Conor asked dryly.

"No, that's all. I swear."

They stepped onto the front porch and Eilwen rapped on the metal frame of the screen door. No answer. "They're at church too, I'll bet." She faced Conor. "You

148

probably shouldn't be here when they get home. It'd be best for me to talk to Dristan alone first."

Conor looked argumentative, but then stared ahead with a forced blank expression and made himself nod. His eyes grew expressive again when he asked, "Where should I go until they get home?"

"Just stay here with me." Eilwen sat on the steps and motioned for him to sit beside her. Conor did so enthusiastically. Then he stood. "Let's sit over here instead. Eilwen, I'm going to touch ya now." He grabbed her hand and led her from the porch. They sat on the split-rail fence around the goat yard. "The porch railing was iron. I was feeling dizzy."

"Does iron hurt everything magic?"

"The more magic you are, the more it hurts ya. Fairies, for example, wouldn't have been able to stand on that porch near as long as I. Unless they took a more mortal form."

"How can one take a *more* mortal form?"

"Deep magic stuff," said Conor dismissively. "More advanced than I've yet studied. That's another controversy: whether to teach it. Mother and the Coven have opposing standings. That's one of the reasons she left."

"What are the other reasons?"

"I dunno. Stupid stuff. Anyway…" Conor rushed, fiddling absently with his sleeve cuffs. "Iron affects you differently depending on your Element. Fires are most sensitive to it. Earth witches are rather sensitive too, iron being earth in a sense."

"And Earth *warlocks*," Eilwen added.

Conor looked pleasantly surprised. "Right."

"Why are Fires most sensitive?"

"Well, our Element is Fire. Energy. Electricity. It's why we're born able to see auras, being most sensitive to electromagnetic fields. And our own fields are frightful sensitive as well. Iron is magnetic. It mangles our aura, twists it up... Fires have been known to pass out or die around too much. Any witch will die around too much iron, but for Fires it's worse. That's why Fires are so rare. We're *too* sensitive. Most don't survive to birth. It's particularly bad in this part of the world, of course, away from the equator."

"What do you mean?"

"Not enough sunlight." Eilwen suddenly noticed that Conor had positioned himself in such a way that he was receiving as much of the morning sun as would sift through the trees; she was reminded of a sunflower, whose bright head eagerly followed the sun across the sky. "Winter's a terrible time for Fires." His voice turned distant. "At first just days go between sightings, then weeks, and soon you've not seen a ray of sun in months. It's painful, as though you're deprived of some crucial vitamin. You feel you'll wither like the flowers. You begin to *want* to wither. Many a Fire have killed themselves on account of winter."

"That's horrible. Conor, why not move south?" Not that Eilwen wanted him to leave.

Conor shrugged. "Why didn't Mother's ancestors leave Ireland? Witches and warlocks are attached to the land they're born to in ways no mundane can understand. Mother told me leaving Ireland was one of the hardest things she'd done in all her life, and she's… well… she's had a great Hell of some experiences."

"Why'd she leave?"

"The war," said Conor. "And my da. And my da bein' in the war." He paused. "And me.

"Mother began carrying me a few months into the Civil War. The Irish one, not your own convoluted affair. She knew she risked losing me as it was, carrying a Fire child, and didn't want the stress of war aiding my death, so she sailed to the States. 'Twas better than going to England. Or Scotland, the shifty bastards. She got to New York in spring of twenty-three, and bore me that July, the very day she arrived in Kentucky. She says that's how she knew she was to stay here. Says it was a sign. That I'd been waiting for her to get here all along."

"Glad you waited. Otherwise I'd have never met you."

"I'm glad as well." Conor positively beamed, then he seemed to grow suddenly nervous and stared ahead again. Eilwen wondered what was wrong.

"Is it the iron?" she asked. "Making you dizzy?"

Conor blushed. "No, not the iron. Anymore."

Eilwen wondered what she would see around Conor right now if she could see auras. "What's my color right now?" she asked.

"Still muddy. You're a hard one to read. I reckon your wicked aunt's to blame. Probably frightened ya into all manner of confusion about who you are and what you feel."

Eilwen regretted asking.

Conor hopped down from the fence suddenly and plucked a piece of grass, then he hopped back up and held the grass out for her to see. "Watch this."

Before Eilwen's eyes, the sprig's green color changed flawlessly to purple. *Purple.* A purple blade of grass. Her mouth fell open. "How'd you do that?"

"Magic." Conor grinned.

"Can I learn?"

"In time." The sprig changed to yellow, pink, sky-blue – the changes so smooth, the eye hardly noticed. "It's one of the simplest tricks, but it is handy! A smart enough witch could go through life only ever using variations of this spell."

"What's the spell?"

"Well, uh, there's no standard one. The core of it's manipulating light waves." The sprig changed again, displaying an awkwardly-striped pattern that contained all the colors of the rainbow, as though there were a prism at work somewhere instead of Conor's fingers. "Normally grass reflects green light. I changed the color being reflected. And now it's reflecting *all* the colors!" He held up the sprig, amused with himself.

"Can you make the whole yard rainbow?" Eilwen asked.

"Not for long. It only lasts as long as I concentrate." The sprig faded back to green. "I tried changin' my hair once but I got distracted and the spell died. *Maime* knows how to make spells stick. She can change the color of our entire house and never have to think about it again."

"Couldn't she change your hair for you?"

"She won't," Conor pouted. "Says I'm beautiful the way I was born or some nonsense."

Eilwen bit her lip; she would have loved to have been denied something out of conviction that she was perfect the way she was.

She rested her head in her hand and watched Conor toy with the sprig's colors, mind adrift, when suddenly the sound of a motorcar reached her. "Truck coming." She slid off the fence. "It's not Aunt's. It might be Dristan. Where will –?" She turned, having been about to ask Conor where he'd be hiding, but he was nowhere to be seen. "Is this another light trick?"

"It is." Conor reappeared behind her. Gracie hissed. "I'll need to be away from the porch. Listen for me, you'll know where I am."

When Dristan and his aunt emerged from the midnight-blue truck that had just parked beside the cottage, everything happened quickly: first was Dristan's yelp at seeing Eilwen, who flinched and stiffened at so suddenly feeling arms around her. "Thank God!" he cried. "Your aunt came looking for you last night! She was so angry! Eilwen, I'd never seen anyone shake with rage!"

"Yeah, she does that." Eilwen awkwardly returned his hug.

"Are you hurt? Where've you been? I spent half the night searching the woods for you! Aunt Thelma, let's get her some food and... oh..." His voice lowered when he noticed Gracie half-coiled in Eilwen's coat. "Thank God you're *both* safe."

"Aunt tried to kill her," Eilwen blurted. The words seemed to vomit out. "With a hoe. Aunt tried to cut Gracie's head off with a hoe." Her voice cracked, but she fought back the tears. It helped, for once, to have Dristan hug her again, for she knew he, having once thought his own Familiar dead, understood her panic.

"I have a lot to talk to you about," she told him quietly as they followed Thelma to the door.

"I'm sure you do."

"About Cicely."

Dristan stopped walking and faced Eilwen, eyes searching.

He led her into his room. Thelma removed her earrings and put them away, then went to the kitchen to prepare Sunday brunch for three people. "I feel bad not helping cook, but I don't think she'll be angry given the circumstances," Dristan said, shutting his door. "She took Cicely well."

Eilwen spun around. "You told her?" In an odd way, she was hurt; she'd thought this her and Dristan's secret.

"Didn't really have a choice." Dristan sank down on his brass-frame bed. "I couldn't leave Cicely out at night. And Aunt Thelma was aware of there being an animal in her house. She was on to me in minutes. There had to be an introduction."

One of his ice-blue pillows moved and Cicely crawled out from the sheets and into his lap. "She was very accepting. Her only concern is feeding her. And other things... But she believed me when I told her Cicely would let me know if she needed out." He looked warmly at the otter, then up at Eilwen. "Should I ask you to start where we left off yesterday, or is there a certain order you want to go in?"

Eilwen took a deep breath. "Do you believe in fairies?"

Dristan blinked rapidly. "I... Do *what?*"

It was the most interesting afternoon of Eilwen's life. She told Dristan everything – from the stories Old Hal had imparted about fairies and clovers, to everything that had happened immediately following Eilwen sending Dristan away yesterday afternoon. She told him of Conor, and the clover, and Ygraine and the Border. She told him that she and Dristan were both magic themselves, deliberately neglecting to mention the words 'witch' or 'warlock' and using instead every compound adjectival noun she could think of in their place; she wondered if Dristan would still have taken this all so collectedly, as he was currently doing, had she deigned to use more truthful titles. When she was through, all she could think was that she was thankful Dristan couldn't see auras.

He was silent, staring at the floor. He sounded like he was about to say something, then stopped, and turned to look out his window. "You know, my mother believed in fairies."

Eilwen's tight chest muscles relaxed. "She did?"

Dristan nodded, his window-turned gaze wistful, as though watching a memory on the panes. The lace curtains cast a white glow. "She told me it was all right to believe in them, because they were angels. Too heavy with sin to remain in Heaven, but not heavy enough to fall all the way to Hell, and so they're here, on this level, with us."

Eilwen was dumbstruck. Perhaps God could love witches after all.

Dristan whispered, "I wonder... did she know something? The way you think your granduncle must have?"

There was a sharp tap on the windowpane.

Gracie hissed.

"Was that a bird?" Dristan slid the curtains aside. Eilwen was about to say she didn't know when she realized that she did. She leapt to the window, almost knocking Dristan aside. "How do you open this?"

"Why are you opening it?" Dristan sounded concerned.

"Just help me."

Dristan undid the locks and helped Eilwen lift the frame. Outside air rushed sweet and soft into the room, and as Eilwen lifted the screen, Conor seemed to materialize out of nowhere, droplets of light and color flashing around him. The illusion's remnants disappeared when Eilwen blinked.

The redheaded warlock looked inquisitively at her. "You told him yet?"

"Just finished. Can you give us a bit longer?"

"I'm bored."

"Eilwen, who is this?" Dristan demanded.

"Just let me in, I won't say anything, I promise," Conor begged. Eilwen sighed and pulled him through the window.

Dristan was gawking. "What the Hell is going on?" he cried. "Excuse me. But... No, what's going on?"

"*Everything all right, Dristan?*" Aunt Thelma's voice reached them, muffled, from down the hall.

"Fine!" called a flustered Dristan. "Just... showing Cicely to Eilwen!"

"I thought I was going to get you when we were finished," Eilwen said to Conor, who sat on the windowsill, legs dangling into Dristan's room. She grew worried. "Is something the matter? Is it one of the dangers we're vulnerable to now?"

Conor gave a very unconvincing shrug.

"Eilwen, who is this?" Dristan flung his arm toward Conor, who moved to stand beside Eilwen.

"Some manners," Conor scoffed. "I'm the one who's saved you and Eilwen from a mundane life of confusion and unfulfillment. Count yourself lucky, most don't ever get saved."

"Eilwen, who is he and what is he blabbering about?"

Conor's brows fell.

"The same thing I was talking to you about," said Eilwen. "Conor's what we are. He's magic too."

Dristan shook his head. "I'm sorry, I just can't get past the fact that you've dragged a stranger into my room through my window. Eilwen, maybe we should think about this... *fairy* nonsense a little more before we –"

"Oh, Dristan, don't! You were so willing to believe me earlier!" Eilwen pleaded. "Conor's my friend. He's the one who found me last night. He's the one who told me everything! And he can do magic. Conor, show him something!"

Conor only glared at Dristan.

"Eilwen, I'm growing very worried, very fast." Dristan's tone was distressingly tempered. He looked at her with such concern that Eilwen nearly let herself believe she was guilty of something.

"I'm – You shouldn't be," she stammered. "You were the one who told me, when we met, that you sensed things. Felt things. You told me even *you* thought you were crazy! And now I have an answer!"

157

"But if the only answer's a crazy one…" Dristan's voice was strained, as though he were only half convinced of both their stances. "And you still haven't answered my biggest question, the one you said you would. What is Cicely? Why do I love her so much? Where'd this spontaneous affection come from?"

"You told me it was scary what love does to the body," said Eilwen steadily, looking at him. "Maybe love itself is just magic."

"I'd be careful arguing with this one," Conor butted in. "She remembers everything she hears. Pity she's a witch, really, she's a lot of lawyer potential from what I've read."

"*Witch?*" Dristan had almost shouted the word but remembered his aunt down the hall and instead furiously whispered it.

Conor threw up his hands. "The stereotype lives!"

"Eilwen, you said –!"

"Because I knew you'd react like this! Yes, I'm a witch." It felt strange – a right sort of strange, though – to say it out loud. "I'm a witch, and so are you."

"Actually, he's a –"

"I know, Conor, but explaining that right now takes away form the –"

"*I'm* a *witch?*" said Dristan.

"Warlock," Conor corrected.

Dristan fell onto his bed.

Eilwen shot Conor a look and Conor backed against the window, head down. She looked pityingly at Dristan, wracking her brain for something comforting to say.

"To answer your question," she began quietly, stepping forward. "Cicely is your Familiar. An animal as magic as you are, born the same time as you. That's why you're so important to each other. You've been meant to be together all your lives."

Dristan's head lifted enough for Eilwen to detect in his eyes a glow of understanding – of relief. Cicely shared that glow. He was silent for some time.

"My mother's way of seeing things was a simple one," he spoke at long last. Eilwen noticed his eyes were bluer – from tears? "She said anything is possible, and that if something seems special, it is. You seemed special to me the moment I saw you, Eilwen, digging through those lilies. I can't help thinking I was meant to find you as well." He said apologetically, "That we were meant to help each other. Thank you, if this is the truth, for shedding light on it for me. I can't tell you how it's plagued me. I knew you were going to be special. Like no one I'd ever met."

Eilwen felt a surge of warmth and flushed, unused to compliments – and what a compliment! She wanted to tell Dristan how much he meant to her. How much meeting him had meant.

Something clattered near the window.

They turned and saw Conor standing over a pile of shattered porcelain. The shards sat amid a pile of fine white dust, as though they lay in their own blood. Conor looked pale. "Was that terribly valuable?"

Dristan's eyes flared. "My aunt's pitcher. What did you do?"

"Dropped it, obviously, but –"

"*Dristan, what was that?*" Thelma's footsteps hurried toward his room.

"Nothing, Aunt Thelma, Cicely's just… getting rambunctious!" Dristan's eyes were fixed, horrified, on the mess. "This'll be the third one I've broken! Or… *he's* broken!"

Thelma replied curtly, *"It didn't sound like nothing! I changed my mind, I don't like the idea of a girl in your room. Bring Eilwen out to the living room and chat there."*

Dristan dashed to his door before Thelma could barge in, poking his head out and uncomfortably fabricating that Eilwen was having a breakdown over what had happened last night and that Thelma entering would worsen it. Eilwen, meanwhile, was kneeling on the floor with Conor. "What happened?" she asked.

"I told you, I dropped it. Accidentally."

"Why were you holding it?"

"No one told me not to touch anything!"

"Can you fix it?"

Conor sighed. "Stand back." He drew what looked like a wand from his tunic.

"Dristan, really, I would feel a lot better if you and Eilwen sat in the living room," Thelma insisted with unusual sternness.

Conor was tracing an invisible line around the pitcher with his wand. His eyes were focused. His mouth moved inaudibly, nonetheless causing the hairs on the back of Eilwen's neck to stand – he was muttering in another language, and though Eilwen couldn't understand the words, she could tell they carried power. She could feel it.

Conor finished speaking and the instant he did so, two things happened: one was that the shards and the dust all flew – instantaneously, as though pulled by a magnet –

back into place, reforming the pitcher with seamless perfection. The other was that Thelma Duvall pushed open the door and burst inside just in time to witness the magical reformation take place.

She shrieked.

Conor and Eilwen looked up, alarmed. Dristan froze, panicked. Gracie coiled in striking position and hissed, terrified. Thelma, despite her horror, had the presence of mind to pull from her apron an iron dagger.

She lunged at Gracie, dagger raised. Eilwen screamed and hurried to protect her Familiar, but Conor was closer, and without a moment's hesitation he threw himself between Thelma and the snake.

The dagger lodged in his upper arm. Conor fell instantly to the floor, unconscious. The blood from his wound pooled around him, and the pitcher fell to pieces.

Chapter VIII

One of Those Melungeons

Three things not easily restrained,
The flow of a torrent,
The flight of an arrow,
And the tongue of a fool.
– "The Welsh Triads"

The air animated in a breeze, whipping up the curtains and bed sheets. "Conor! Oh my God, what did you do? CONOR! Oh my God, that was iron, wasn't it? What did you do?"

Eilwen rolled Conor over and tried to wake him. The fact that she could hear his breath was the only reason she did not fall to pieces any more than she already was. "Conor! Conor, wake up, please!" She pulled the dagger from his arm and felt suddenly dizzy. She tossed it weakly across the room. "Conor, it's out! Wake up, please!"

"Aunt Thelma!" Dristan breathed. He was frozen near the door. Gracie had fled under his bed with Cicely.

Thelma was backed against a dresser, face falling from horrified maternal ire to something more unreadable as the confusing scene began to dawn on her. "Who is this?" she demanded. Her knuckles were white she gripped the dresser so tightly. "Dristan! Do you know him? What's he doing in our house?"

"Is he all right?" Dristan asked Eilwen, instead of answering his aunt, for he had no simple answer for her.

162

"I don't know!" Tears formed in her eyes as she tried to shake Conor awake. His head lolled. "You stabbed him with iron! You tried to kill Gracie! Why'd you try to kill her?"

"I was protecting Dristan!" Thelma's voice shook.

"Let's at least stop the bleeding." Dristan seemed to be coming back to himself, though his eyes remained wide. "I'll get some wet rags. Aunt Thelma, help me. I'll explain what I can."

Eilwen stayed with Conor, begging him to wake up, while Dristan and a still-shaking Thelma left for rags and water. Gracie emerged from beneath the bed and slithered up to Conor, softly nosing his cheek.

She coiled herself protectively above Conor's head after Dristan, Thelma and Eilwen moved the unconscious warlock onto Dristan's bed, and there she remained, eyeing Thelma threateningly. Eilwen had kept Gracie at bay long enough for Thelma and Dristan to clean and wrap the deep gash in Conor's arm; they had had to rewrap it several times, for the blood kept soaking through. Eventually – it took a far longer time than usual, which made them all worry – the blood flow slowed, and only crimson spots here and there showed through the cloth. Eilwen and Dristan began mopping up the blood on the floor with the remaining rags while Thelma sat motionlessly in a rocking chair in the corner, Cicely in her lap.

"As soon as Dristan introduced me to this otter last night, I knew it was a Familiar." Thelma's statement broke what had been a very long silence.

Eilwen and Dristan stared at her, speechless.

"And then I realized that that snake you all found lying next to Eilwen the other day must have been *her* Familiar."

Eilwen felt as though her insides had dropped away.

Dristan slowly stood. "Aunt Thelma..."

"Nothing good could come of that." Thelma spoke directly to Eilwen and ignored her nephew. "You're a sweet girl, Eilwen. But Dristan's the only family I got left. A witch with a black snake... it just sounds bad, don't it? And I wanted to be a good Christian and give you the benefit of the doubt, but as soon as Dristan invited you in today, I went straight to my room and grabbed that knife. Just to be safe was all. When I heard the racket, I feared he was in danger. Figured something suspicious was going under, and damn it if I didn't walk in to see some red-haired stranger in my house magicking away at my porcelain! It just looked bad, all right? And that snake. It just looked bad. I didn't mean to hurt anyone. Didn't expect that boy to jump in the way. Wasn't sure he *was* a boy, or human. He just looks *magic*."

Thelma glanced at Conor. Gracie shivered her tail.

"Aunt Thelma, how do you know what a Familiar is?" Dristan choked out. Then, angrily, "And why didn't you tell me?"

Thelma sniffed and rocked once in the chair. "Your mother was a witch. Water witch. Same as you."

Thelma began bawling. Dristan glared at her with his mouth agape, but rushed to her side and took her hands; it seemed to be against his nature to refuse comfort to anyone in tears, even someone with whom he was outraged. "You knew how much it was bothering me!" he accused, the look on his face betraying how much he hated

164

speaking to his aunt in such a way. "You knew and didn't say anything! How long did Mom know? Are you a witch, too?" Dristan suddenly released his aunt's hands, almost throwing them down. "How long did you both know?"

Thelma winced at her nephew's indignation. "From the time Cicely was thirteen. Back when we were growing up in Louisville. She found that mangy housecat of hers on Fourth Street near Central Park – or rather, it found her. A few months later, a red-haired woman in a blue coat approached us while we were playing in the park. Started asking questions. Talking to us in an odd way. I was getting frightened and wanted Cicely to take me home, but Cissie was taking a shine to this woman. Their talk got odder and odder still until the woman finally out and told Cicely she wasn't human, but a *witch*, of all things! Sweet, saintly Cicely, who looked forward to Mass every Sunday, who'd had every prayer of the rosary memorized before she could walk, was a *witch*.

"Well, I thought this woman hysterical. I grabbed Cissie's arm, but she wouldn't budge. She was giving this stranger's claim consideration! And wasn't the least bit offended by the idea! Soon Cicely was a regular visitor at her house – some ritzy, superstitious mansion on Third Street that was supposedly haunted – and would come home every evening practicing spells and incantations and chants in languages long dead. Not just Latin, but Old English, and Welsh and whatnot. Her powers were never good, since like every other witch in Louisville she was disadvantaged living in the city. But she knew her stuff. Knew the mechanics, if nothing else. She met your father through the Louisville Coven. Air warlock. Married him

165

a few years later.

"Then I married your uncle and moved out here. Cissie always loved visiting us. She loved the countryside. Said she always felt sick in the city, but she'd grown up with it, so came to view her sickliness as normal. It's the iron, of course. Every building in Louisville has iron frames. She wanted to move out here but couldn't make herself leave the river. She was always sentimental. Even during the flood, she refused to leave. When her own Element sickened her, all the iron in the city kept her from recovering. That and the grief from losing her husband. It's a miracle you survived, Dristan. You're every bit as magic as she was and so have to be just as vulnerable. I reckon she gave her life using what little magic she could to keep you healthy."

Dristan stormed out of the room without another word. He slammed the door behind him.

Thelma let her face fall into her hands.

Eilwen wanted to go after Dristan but did not want to leave Conor, nor leave him and Gracie alone with the woman who had brandished an iron weapon against them barely an hour ago. She also knew that as upset as Dristan was, her priority right now had to be Conor's health. Eilwen had to get him back to Ygraine as soon as possible.

"Miss Thelma," she said. "Do you have a horse I can borrow?"

Thelma was all too willing to assist Eilwen in any way she could. She showed her to the barn and equipped her with an old bridal and saddle, then pointed Eilwen to a field where two mares grazed. Eilwen approached the closer, praying the horse did not respond to her in the vicious manner Mahitabel had yesterday, and was relieved when the animal allowed her to both touch and tack her. Thelma waited at the gate, opening and closing it for Eilwen as she led the horse out. "I'm so sorry," she said.

Eilwen had mixed feelings, being angry at Thelma for what she had done to both Dristan and Conor and for what she'd attempted to do to Gracie, but also understanding of the genuine remorse in her tone. She simply nodded. "I'll bring the horse back when I can."

Thelma helped Eilwen carry Conor outside and heave him onto the horse, positioning him upright so that Eilwen could sit behind him and hold him steady. Gracie had tucked herself away in Eilwen's coat to avoid startling the animal. "Where do you think Dristan is?" Eilwen asked before leaving.

"In the woods, I expect. Near the creek." Thelma looked at Eilwen. "I wanted to tell him. I saw him suffering. But it wasn't my secret to tell."

"His parents are *dead*," Eilwen responded. "Who else was he supposed to learn it from?"

She kicked the horse toward Lily Lane. As she rode, the notion that Old Hal might have known what Eilwen was all this time resurfaced; when the thought first occurred to her this morning it had been comforting and exciting, but now it bothered her. What if he really *had* known? And if he had known anything, had he not owed Eilwen the truth every bit as much as Thelma had owed Dristan?

* * *

The horse – Thelma had said her name was Constance – was cooperative, understanding on some intuitive animal level that the task at hand was not frivolous. Her steps were speedy but careful. Eilwen had been worried about riding a horse through the crowded woods, but it had been a relief to duck into the trees: thunder had rumbled seconds after leaving Lily Lane, and she'd just barely avoided getting soaked.

Rain pattered on the leaves. Eilwen removed her coat. "Sorry, Gracie," she said, wrapping it around Conor. But Gracie simply slithered into the coat and snuggled with Conor instead.

Eilwen tried to remember the way through the trees. She had been counting on Conor's presence to access the parts of the forest hidden by the Border, but hadn't considered his cognizance might be necessary. What if she walked in circles? What if she never found Ygraine, and Conor died from iron poisoning, as he'd said Fires often did? Eilwen held him close to reassure herself he was still breathing.

The sound of it whizzing through the air came first.

Pain exploded in Eilwen's left shoulder as she was thrown from the horse to the ground. Constance whinnied, but calmed suddenly. Eilwen, whose breath had been knocked out of her, tried to cry out but couldn't. The arrow that had pierced her quivered as her breath slowly returned.

She was on her back. Her shoulder burned. Her shirt was wet with blood.

It was then she heard footsteps. She turned her head and saw Conor, still unconscious, lying against a tree a few yards away. Someone was tying Constance to a low hanging branch.

"Hey!" Eilwen shouted. She moved to sit up, but was stopped.

"Don't move!" A second person stood over her, aiming an arrow directly at her face.

Eilwen nearly screamed. "What's going on?" she panicked, then remembered what Conor had told her about how magical creatures protected these woods. "I'm sorry, I think I'm lost!"

The girl wielding the bow and arrow narrowed her moss-green eyes. She was wearing a soiled and sweaty fringed hunting shirt, and boots that looked like moccasins. A loaded quiver was slung across her torso. "Don't play dumb. Why was this boy in your possession? Where were you taking him?"

Eilwen stared in fear, lost for words.

The girl jerked the arrow threateningly. "Speak!"

"I – I need to find Ygraine! The boy's mother. He's sick and he needs her help!" Eilwen grimaced; her shoulder was on fire.

"And just *how* did he get sick?" demanded the girl.

"Stabbed with iron."

The girl's expression waned. Eilwen heard a creak and winced in fear as the bowstring loosened ever so slightly.

"Did she say *iron?*"

The person who had been tethering Constance approached them. She was young as well, dressed similarly, but possessed jet-black hair and skin as brown as Eilwen's. Instead of a bow and arrow, she held what looked like a single dried tube of river cane. "That explains why his arm's bandaged."

"Didn't want to leave a trail of blood to follow. What

coven are you from? Are you rogue? Who are you working for?"

"I – nowhere!" Eilwen stammered. "I'm not from a coven, I'm trying to help my friend!"

"How a mundane managed to get close enough to a Fire to use iron on him is beyond me. You had help from someone. What do you need this boy for? Who sent you?"

"He's my friend! I'm a witch, like him!" Eilwen whimpered as she tried to sit up, but the arrow – both the one in her shoulder and the one being aimed at her – kept her from moving. "He was visiting another friend of mine and got hurt." She didn't feel it wise to impart that the person who'd stabbed Conor had been her other friend's relation.

"If you're taking him to his mother, why are you riding in the opposite direction?"

"I told you, I'm lost."

"At least *try* to come up with a better story!" The girl turned to her companion. "Ayasta, go get help. I'll keep an eye on her."

The other girl was just making to untie Constance when Eilwen, grasping at a sudden flicker of hope, cried, "Ayasta! You're Conor's friend, aren't you?"

Ayasta paused.

"Don't try pulling anything." The bowstring creaked as the girl pulled it tighter.

"No, Conor told me about you!" Eilwen pleaded to Ayasta, ignoring the other girl in her desperation. "You told him he couldn't have seen an underwater panther because they only live in the Great Lakes!"

Ayasta stopped moving and stared at Eilwen.

"I'm not lying!" Eilwen urged. Her eyes darted between her two captors. "Can't you see my aura?"

"What do I look like, a Fire?"

"She might be a witch," the girl named Ayasta conceded thoughtfully. "Look at her eyes. Yellow, like mine."

"She could just be a drunk. Bad liver and all. Ain't that why it's illegal for mundanes to drink?"

"Prohibition stopped four years ago," Ayasta informed exasperatedly.

"*How* do you *know* that?" said the girl, almost annoyed.

"I pay attention to what goes on out*side* the Border, unlike *some* people."

"Why on earth do you care what goes on out there?"

"Just because we're isolated from the rest of the world doesn't mean we shouldn't care what goes on in it. The Uktena Child happened because of that!"

The girl seemed to relent at this. Then she shook her head and said, "Just go!"

Ayasta looked once more at Eilwen, then untied Constance. The horse allowed her to mount without any objection at all, and she rode her easily away into the trees.

Eilwen snorted. "'Constance' my ass —"

"Hush," snapped the girl. "No talking." Her yellow hair was short and fluffy, bouncing when she yanked the bowstring tighter.

For a time, the only sounds were the birdsongs amid the patter of raindrops on the damp earth and mossy branches. And the deafening pounding of Eilwen's heart in her own ears. She shut her eyes, trying to block the scorching pain in her shoulder, then turned her head and watched Conor, thankful beyond words Gracie had not been on her person when the arrow had been fired. She could see the snake's yellow eyes, leering from the coat's sleeve, beneath Conor's hand. His hidden guardian.

Eilwen wished she could tell Gracie *Good girl*.

"If he dies," said the archer suddenly, for she had been watching Eilwen gaze at Conor, "I'll kill you."

Eilwen swallowed, then looked up and met her captor's eyes. "I was about to say the same to you."

The girl's eyes widened infinitesimally.

Minutes later, Eilwen felt the tremor of horse hooves beating the earth. Constance burst from amid the massive trees, driven not by Ayasta, but by Ygraine Sheehan.

The Irish Fire witch flew from the horse before even reaching a halt and raced to her unconscious son. "Ivy, lower your bow," she commanded without even looking at the girl.

The girl obediently lowered her weapon. Eilwen, relieved, turned to watch Ygraine, who stroked Conor's face and whispered tenderly to him in Irish. The rag bandaging his arm was soaked red again. Ygraine placed a hand on it and muttered something, then called Ivy over. Eilwen watched as Ygraine ordered her onto Constance and handed Conor's limp body into her arms. Ivy carried Conor away into the trees, holding him in front of her the same way Eilwen had done only a little while ago.

Gracie had slithered out of the coat before Conor had been handed off, and was now beside Eilwen, hovering frantically near the arrow. Eilwen wanted to comfort her, for she could feel her worry. She wanted to reassure her she'd be all right. But truthfully, Eilwen didn't know. She had slaughtered her fair share of animals; she knew all too well the lasting damage of a bloodletting blow.

Ygraine hurried to Eilwen. "Can you move your arm at all?"

Eilwen nodded. "It hurts to."

"That'll pass. At least you can move it. Hold still and try not to scream." Ygraine pinched the shaft of the arrow between her thumb and forefinger and attempted to twist it. Eilwen felt a searing pain in her collar and jerked. "Damn," Ygraine breathed. "It's in the bone."

Eilwen sucked in air through her teeth. Tears welled in her eyes. Ygraine placed a hand over the wound and around the arrow and pressed, muttering in another language.

Eilwen gasped, but was alarmed when the pain vanished – or rather, significantly decreased. "I'm calming the nerves around the wound," Ygraine explained, sensing Eilwen's confusion. "They've done their duty. They've informed you you're damaged. They're resting now while I pull out the arrow. I beg ya not squirm. This shouldn't hurt *much*, but it'll be mighty uncomfortable."

Ygraine pulled from her belt a knife of bone. Tearing the hole in Eilwen's shirt, she lowered the knife to her skin and cut into the flesh around the entry wound, widening it. Eilwen gasped as she watched yet more of her own blood well across her collar.

"I'll stop the bleeding when I'm finished," Ygraine assured monotonously, rusty eyes fixed on the incision.

Though the pain was minimal, it was all Eilwen could do to keep from squirming – it felt unnatural not to when you could feel something calmly cutting into you, pain or no.

Finally, Ygraine pulled the knife from the wound. She wiped her hands on her dress before taking the arrow in her grip. "When I say so, pull away from me," she ordered. Eilwen whimpered, but nodded, and at Ygraine's command, pushed back hard against the forest floor just as Ygraine pulled with all her might. Eilwen felt her collarbone vibrate as the arrowhead dislodged. Ygraine nearly stumbled backwards. "Damn lucky," she said, and tossed the arrow to the ground. "There's only one good place to get hit in the shoulder, and Ivy hit it. Your clover's rubbed off on you."

Ygraine placed her hand over the wound. She muttered again in a foreign tongue, and Eilwen felt a tingling in her shoulder. The bleeding stopped.

Ygraine mopped up what blood had already escaped with the remains of Eilwen's shirt, then lifted her into her arms. She carried Eilwen through the forest, all the way to the glade where hid the Sheehans' cottage. Gracie slithered speedily alongside.

The rain had picked up. Thunder rumbled. By the time Ygraine reached her front door, she and Eilwen were soaked.

Ivy and Ayasta had laid Conor on the sofa and scooted it against the fireplace. Molly lay on his chest, nosing his face.

Ygraine set Eilwen in a chair, then disappeared into a bedroom off the side of the sitting area before returning. She'd prepared a hot, soapy bath in a large wooden bin beside her bed, and told Eilwen to soak for as long as she wanted. "I enchanted it to keep hot, and there are fresh clothes on my bed when you're finished. Take your time, dear." Ygraine left and shut the door.

Eilwen climbed shakily into the wooden washtub, the hot water shocking but soothing. Gracie slithered into the water as well, and Eilwen relaxed watching her slip under and about the surface like a black sea serpent.

She tried not to look at her wound. She did not attempt to clean around it until she'd kept her shoulder submerged a good half hour. She was in disbelief that the bleeding had ceased so absolutely; after drying, she hesitated before donning the new clothes, and was extraordinarily careful when she finally did.

She exited Ygraine's room. The cottage was warm and silent, the only sound the crackling fire. Ygraine had moved the sofa enough away from the hearth that she could sit on the floor and caress Conor's face. When she saw Eilwen, she beckoned her over. "Stay with him," she said, and stood. "I need to wash and change. There's food on the table, but keep at his side while you eat, if you will."

Eilwen nodded, and Ygraine disappeared into her room.

Eilwen studied Conor's sleeping face, stomach trembling. He was like this right now because of her. Because he had saved Gracie. She practically fell to the floor in her urgency to sit near him. "Conor, I'm going to touch you now," she whispered, and slid her hand into his, though it did not grip back.

Thunder rumbled.

It occurred to Eilwen that Conor needed sunlight. He would not get it until the rain passed. Idly, she wondered if Dristan's fury was not behind this downpour; it was obvious Eilwen's own moods influenced the wind. It had been wind that saved herself and Gracie from Mona.

The front door unlatched.

Ayasta cautiously entered, followed more cautiously by Ivy. Eilwen watched in silence, unsure what to do or say. She tightened her grip on Conor's hand.

Ayasta glanced at Ivy, who looked awkward and subdued, then stepped toward Eilwen. *"Tsalagis hiwonisgi?"* she asked.

Eilwen swallowed. "What?"

"Do you speak *Tsalagis*?" Ayasta stepped closer. "Cherokee."

"Oh. No." Eilwen added hastily, "I'm sorry."

"You're one of those Melungeons, aren't you?"

Eilwen blinked, not wanting to discuss the matter now. "I... don't know."

Ayasta nodded pensively. She beckoned Ivy over.

The archer hesitantly complied. "I'm sorry I shot you," she said to Eilwen, uncomfortably but not inauthentically. She looked terribly small and young all of a sudden. Eilwen wondered how old she was.

She blankly nodded, unused to having anyone who'd ever caused her harm apologize for it. Gracie slithered onto Conor's chest beside Molly and coiled in striking position, hissing at Ivy, who made a face and inched backwards. "Is this your snake?" she asked. She sounded as though she were attempting to sound conversational while also looking for answers. "I saw it slip out of Conor's coat. While I was riding away, I wondered if you were telling the truth about being a witch, and if the snake was your Familiar."

176

Eilwen nodded again. "She is."

"How come she's grown already?"

Eilwen paused.

"So you say you're a witch, but you're not from a coven. Your Familiar isn't the same age as you. And you were carrying one of the only Fire warlocks in the state unconscious toward mundane territory."

"Ivy, shush it!" Ayasta frowned at her. "Ygraine trusts her."

"I'm not saying I don't trust her, *exactly*," Ivy blushed, glancing repentantly at the ground, "I'm just saying it's all mighty confusing."

"I didn't know I was a witch until last night," Eilwen explained. "Conor found me and told me what I was. He came with me to talk to a friend I thought might be magic too, and got hurt protecting Gra – my snake from someone. I was trying to bring him to Ygraine, but couldn't remember the way."

"You were mundane-raised?"

Eilwen couldn't tell if Ivy was shocked or angry. "Our farm's just outside the Border," she offered, hoping this made her situation the least bit more acceptable. Not that she particularly cared if the girl who'd put an arrow in her approved of her upbringing.

Ayasta's eyes widened. "You're a tobacco farmer?"

"Along with everyone else in Kentucky." Eilwen chuckled nervously, then cleared her throat and looked at Conor. She wished he would wake up. It suddenly occurred to her how effortlessly she had gotten along with him. She had hardly known him a day, but had felt more comfortable with Conor during the few hours she'd known him than she'd ever felt with people she'd known all her life. He was the first human being since Old Hal with whom she had never worried about being herself. He was the fairy who had stepped out of the trees and made the whole world better right when she'd needed it most. Worry that he might never open his eyes again made a lump form in her throat.

"Hey," Ayasta said softly.

She rushed over to Eilwen and knelt beside her, placing a reassuring arm around her. (When Eilwen started at the unexpected touch, Ayasta assumed it was because she'd agitated her shoulder.) "He'll be all right," she told her. "Everyone magic has some run-in with iron. It's unavoidable these days. I've seen folks come back from worse."

"But he's a Fire," Eilwen choked.

"As soon as the sun's out, he'll be right as rain."

* * *

It had been a full moon last night.

Ygraine explained, while poring over several books later that afternoon, that the three days of the lunar cycle when the moon was at her most powerful were the night she was full, the night preceding, and the night following. "Even if we see no sun, we may still luck into moonlight tonight," she summarized. Though she proceeded to spend much of the rest of the day anticipating the need to prepare spells and concoctions should moonlight fail.

By later afternoon, Eilwen, Ivy and Ayasta were on the floor near the fire, Eilwen having never left Conor's side, and only having eaten because Ivy had periodically and wordlessly brought her bits of food. Ayasta spent most of her time helping Ygraine with whatever research or chores she needed done, occasionally stopping to ask Eilwen how she felt, inquiring about her in a friendly way; her eyes tended to swing toward Eilwen and Conor's clasped hands, and she nodded thoughtfully a lot.

"How can moonlight help a Fire?" Eilwen asked Ygraine when she passed near the sofa on her way to shelve a book.

"Moonlight is just another form of sunlight. Not as strong, but there is strength in softness that can be found nowhere else. The softer approach takes longer, but is far more powerful."

"So if Eilwen's Familiar's already grown, does that mean she'll die young?" Ivy asked.

Ayasta smacked the back of her head.

"I doubt it," Ygraine responded dryly.

"I'm just curious is all," Ivy defended. "I never heard of this before. What do you think it means?"

"I think Eilwen's worried enough as it is without us chatting about the likelihood of her death." With that, it was understood Ygraine had closed the conversation.

Eilwen looked at Gracie, draped around her neck, head raised and observing Connor. Eilwen could not fight the feeling that despite Gracie's outwardly mature appearance, her wide and gleaming eyes revealed an excitable nature that was entirely youthful. If Gracie was a full-grown snake – and indeed, she appeared to be – perhaps she was like Hal: physically adult, but very much a child within.

A half hour later, Ygraine took Eilwen's spot beside Conor and insisted she get up and walk around. "You've been at his side for hours. I'll watch him while you're gone. It's only sprinkling now, go out and stretch your legs. Get some air."

Eilwen reluctantly obeyed. She stepped outside and stared at the wildflower garden, watching the leaves and blossoms flicker under sparse raindrops. A few minutes later, Ivy joined her, bow and quiver slung around her person.

"I'll show you where Constance is," was all she said.

She led Eilwen around the side of the cottage to the barn beyond the vegetable patch. Past the barn, stretching to the other end of the glade, was a small fenced paddock containing several horses. Constance was among them, comfortably socializing, occasionally prancing in the rain.

Eilwen stepped onto the first beam of the fence and rested her head on her hands on the top, thoughts adrift.

Ivy joined her. "It ain't nothing to be ashamed of, you know."

Eilwen looked at her. "My Familiar being grown?"

"No, not that." Ivy shook her head. "Honestly, I'd be nervous as Hell if I were in your shoes that way. Never heard of that happening before." Her eyes widened and she shook her head again, punctuating the abnormality. Eilwen's stomach churned. Then Ivy seemed to notice Eilwen's distress, and quickly amended, "But I meant being a Melungeon. That's nothing to be ashamed of."

"Well, easy for you to say, 'cause you're not in my shoes *that* way, either." Eilwen eyed Ivy coldly and turned away, no longer caring how young the child was.

It had been a long, trying day: she had just found out she was a witch; she had also found out she had an as-of-yet unheard-of age problem with her Familiar; one of the first human friends she'd had in years had been stabbed this morning; and shortly after, she had been shot in the shoulder with an arrow. And now the girl who had loosed said arrow was trying to tell Eilwen she had nothing to fret about regarding something she'd been given every reason to fret about all her life? How *dare* she!

Eilwen remembered the countless times she had been shamed for her skin – for her perpetually "dirty" face and features. *Be good, or the Melungeons will get you* was a threat heard so often in her school it seemed a second name anymore, and the teachers' eyes would linger on her while they said it.

This girl – even if she thought she was helping – had no right to be so presumptuous about what she knew nothing about.

But Ivy responded casually, "Yeah, I am. I'm one, too."

Eilwen's brows furrowed. Had she heard right? She studied the girl. Even in the overcast light, Ivy's skin glowed ivory white.

"My whole family's Melungeon," Ivy went on, shockingly blasé, as though it were something to brag about instead of cover up. She removed her bow and began fiddling with the string. "They all look like you, too. Ma, pa, everyone. Brown skin, dark hair. I'm the black sheep of the family. Or... the *white* sheep, I guess. Don't mean I'm not one of them, though." She pulled her bowstring back, as though taking a shot, though she'd notched no arrow.

Eilwen watched her, silent. "Is your whole family magic?" she asked at last, for Ivy's words had shocked her so, she was uncertain how else to respond.

"Yep." Ivy eased the bowstring back into place.

"What kind of witch are you?"

"Earth. Ayasta's Air, like you."

"Is she a Melungeon, too?"

"Nah, she's Cherokee. Her family's lived within the Border since the coven was created. Her ancestors knew one of the witches who founded it." Ivy slung her bow back over her shoulder and joined Eilwen on the fence. "She and Conor are buddies. That's why we got worried when we saw him getting carried off by a stranger. It was more than just protecting a Fire. We were protecting our friend."

Eilwen nodded. "I understand," she said softly.

"How's your shoulder?" Ivy rushed through the words, as though she were uncomfortable saying them but still felt compelled to ask.

Eilwen nodded again. "It's fine," she assured her.

Apparently satisfied, Ivy relaxed a good deal.

The rain picked up again, and Eilwen and Ivy returned to the cottage. As they walked inside, Eilwen said, "You're a good shot, by the way."

The little girl smiled at her.

Chapter IX

Hidden Light

I saw the different things you did,
But always you yourself you hid.
I felt you push, I heard you call,
I could not see yourself at all –
O wind, a-blowing all day long,
O wind, that sings so loud a song.
– Robert Louis Stevenson, "The Wind"

When the sun started to set, it was still cloudy, and a frustrated Ygraine ordered Eilwen and Ayasta to follow her outside as soon as they finished dinner. "I'll help as much as I can, but you two have the strongest natural affinity for Air. Ivy is Air's opposite, so she'll stay with Conor."

"What are we doing?" Eilwen whispered to Ayasta as they hurried to follow Ygraine's quick strides around to an empty paddock behind the house.

Ygraine answered, "We're blowing these ruddy clouds away so my little boy will wake up."

Eilwen nearly stopped walking. Had she heard right? Ygraine surely wasn't expecting *Eilwen* – who had never intentionally performed magic in her life, and who had not even known she was a witch a full twenty-four hours yet – to assist in *magic*. And surely not on such a grand scale her first time.

Was she?

"You've nothing to fear, Eilwen," Ygraine spoke, as though aware of Eilwen's thoughts. (Eilwen wondered panickingly just how much privacy she had when in the presence of a Fire witch.) "You've been unconsciously manipulating your Element since before you could talk, no doubt. All that's changing now is *intent*. You're aware of what you're doing tonight, and that'll make all the difference."

Ygraine reached the middle of the empty paddock and gazed up at the still, stony sky. The clouds were barely moving – they hung like hardening cement, stretching from treeline to treeline. She looked at Eilwen, then back at the sky. "Tell me which way the wind is blowing."

Eilwen wondered if this was a trick. "Is it… is it even blowing at all?"

"I don't know. Is it?"

"Don't think." Ayasta, who was only a year older than Eilwen but somehow seemed ten years her senior, nodded encouragingly at her. "It's your Element. You're an Air witch – a walking weathervane. You know the wind's state at all times. Thinking about it will mess you up. Just feel it."

Eilwen took a deep breath and closed her eyes, fearing any glance at the motionless treetops or stationary clouds would figuratively cloud her judgment. She was silent, lost in that chaotic initial struggle to not think, aware she was thinking about trying not to think. It was not until this inner stalemate was tipped by the ever so slight realization – a gut instinct – that Gracie, perched on her shoulder, was focusing on the wind as well, that the answer appeared as instinctively to Eilwen as though there were suddenly some nerve in her body designed to gauge the wind and report directly to her brain. A nerve that had always been there, that Eilwen had never voluntarily accessed before. She could almost feel a section of her mind light up. A flame – a surge of energy – had been ignited.

Eilwen pointed in the direction in which her gut told her the air was moving at its glacial pace, then opened her eyes.

Ygraine was smiling at her.

Eilwen smiled too, cautiously proud of herself.

"Both of you focus on helping the air," Ygraine commanded. "Hasten it in the direction in which it already floats; do not force it in another. Air is adaptation. Communicate with your Element in this way – in its own language – and it will listen more."

Eilwen and Ayasta closed their eyes, and already Eilwen felt a surge in the air; an energy that filled her. A breeze brushed them, seeming to have come from nowhere.

Her stomach flipped.

The breeze strengthened. Her hair lifted. She tilted back her head, spreading her arms as the wind gathered and rushed past her.

A laugh escaped her as the air kissed her neck. It was both warm and wet, carrying the scent of leaves, pine needles, and somehow also fresh, untainted nighttime all at once. The sound it made as it rushed over treetops – up and down, bending through branches – was euphoric. Gracie stretched high, as though she, too, could not possibly enjoy the gust enough. The energy was palpable. It seemed to respond to Eilwen's laugh as a puppy does to a smiling face; it surged stronger, whipping her hair.

Ayasta said, "It's working!"

Eilwen opened her eyes and looked up.

Indeed, the sheet of clouds was moving with the wind. Low in the sky a white orb glowed, fighting to shine through.

Eilwen thought of Conor and closed her eyes again. She knew all she had to do was allow the air to realize Conor's importance to her and it would gladly complete the task. Minutes later, she heard Ygraine cry, "Excellent!" and opened her eyes.

Moonlight showered the glade. Silently, the world was bathed in silver.

Ygraine carried Conor outside. "He's not heavy, he's just so damned tall," she muttered as she struggled to reach the middle of the moonlit field. Eilwen rushed to help her lay him in the grass, which Ygraine had magically dried.

"Let us know when he wakes up?" Ayasta said. She and Ivy stood over Eilwen, Ygraine and the sleeping Conor. "We need to be going. We'll pray for him, all of us."

Ygraine promised she would send Sheba to them at the first sign of Conor's waking, then Ivy and Ayasta bid them farewell. Eilwen was barely aware they had left, though.

She watched Conor, waiting. For something. Some sign he was improving. In her worried reverie, she realized what it was about Conor that gave him such an ethereal, fairy-like appearance: it was his complete and utter lack of freckles. He was the whitest boy she'd ever met, with the brightest, reddest hair... yet his skin was as flawless as a blueblood's. Ygraine's as well. Was this a trait of Fires? Were they so immune to sun damage that they developed not even the tiniest freckle?

186

"The moon's out, Conor," Eilwen told him.

She did not remember Ygraine was present until the Fire witch knelt on Conor's other side. Molly bounded into her lap. "What exactly happened?" Ygraine asked.

Eilwen explained how Dristan's aunt had tried to kill Gracie, and how Conor had leaped in the way. As she finished, tears welled in her eyes. "He'll be okay, right?"

"Of course he will." The certainty with which Ygraine responded reassured Eilwen, but she could not seem to keep from crying for some reason. Molly trilled and stepped across Conor's chest, pawing at her. Eilwen sat up and the kitten crawled into her lap.

Eilwen sniffed and wiped her cheek. She was holding Old Hal's cat. His little Mittens was curled in her lap, the same way she had once curled up in his. Did Molly remember the old man? Would she grieve at all to learn of his passing? Had he meant as much to her as she had to him?

"You're a powerful witch, Eilwen," Ygraine said.

Eilwen looked at her.

"Your Element responds to you loyally. Yet you were raised and reared mundane." Ygraine looked directly at Eilwen, instead of at what floated around her. She studied her face, her eyes. Ygraine's expression was almost, Eilwen thought fearfully, concerned. "And I believe I mentioned to ya that only unusually gifted individuals possess snakes as Familiars."

"I've always loved the wind," Eilwen said, somehow feeling as though she had to defend herself. Was it bad to be powerful?

"Do you know what magic is, Eilwen?" Ygraine asked after a moment. Eilwen, wondering if this was another trick question, gave no response. "'Tis not an additional something with which a body's born. It's not an extra. It's a *deficit*. You're frightful sensitive, aren't ya, dear? Have been all your life?"

Eilwen nodded. Gracie looped tighter around her neck.

"Felt things more deeply? Words touched you deeper. Sounds, smells, sights and textures that bothered no one else seemed to bother you greatly. You were thin-skinned. Physically and emotionally. When you felt something, you felt the full of it. You lacked the filter – the thickness of skin that protected everyone else from feeling so intensely as you.

"That's what magic is, Eilwen. That lack of filter. In a magic person, the veil between the inner self and outer world is so thin, they overlap, interacting on a deep level mundanes rarely, if ever, experience. But just as the outer world can deeply touch a magic person's inner self, so too can that inner self affect the world. A magic person's thoughts and feelings flow out into the world with ease. When those thoughts and feelings are channeled and focused with language, that's what we call a *spell*."

Eilwen sat in silence, remembering every instance in her life that vouched for the truth of Ygraine's words. Hal had known she was sensitive. Hal had been the only human being – aside from Conor – who had acknowledged and respected that. "Is it possible," Eilwen asked, "for a person to be only a little magic? To have just a bit of a filter?"

"Indeed, it happens often. Magic is a spectrum. What determines if a body is witch or mundane is where on the spectrum one falls. There is no black and white."

Eilwen stroked Molly, who gazed up at her and purred. That would explain it. Why Hal had known about magic – been sensitive to it – but never possessed a Familiar. Never been a full warlock. Hal T. Hittle had been born on the spectrum same as Eilwen, just not in the same place. He couldn't have owed her the truth about what she was. It was unlikely he had even known.

"Which was why my son worried for ya so." Ygraine stroked Conor's cheek. "When a full witch is born to mundane circumstances, she withers. Often kills herself, if her world doesn't kill her first. 'Tis a double-edged sword, bein' so powerful. The stronger your magic – the stronger your connection to the outer world – the more vulnerable you are to all the ways the world can hurt ya.

"That's why it's so important witches find out what they are. *Who* they are. Learning about yourself – accepting your abilities and weaknesses – strengthens your resolve. Helps you rise above the hurt the world throws at ya. When you see something for what it is, it's easier to handle. You may not see the light at the end of a tunnel, but if you understand the tunnel isn't straight, it's easier to remember the light is there, isn't it?"

Close to an hour passed. Conor made no sign of waking. But neither did the clouds show signs of re-covering the moon. Ygraine announced she would venture back inside for some of the things she believed might assist her son's recovery, and Eilwen swore to stay at his side. "If I can

189

trust him with anyone, it's you, dear," Ygraine said warmly as she stood to leave.

Eilwen was glad it was dark, for she blushed, then wondered if it mattered; could Fires read auras in the dark? Nevertheless, she waited until Ygraine had disappeared before laying beside Conor. Molly and Gracie began meandering about the silver grass, playfully gauging each other. They began a haphazard game of chase. Eilwen could feel Gracie's enjoyment and was glad she was having fun.

A weak groan escaped Conor's throat.

Eilwen jerked up. "Conor?"

Silence.

She moved closer to him. His chest moved quicker, but his eyes remained closed. Minutes passed before he gave any further sign of life. He groaned again and his lips moved. He was muttering so faintly that Eilwen was not even aware he wasn't speaking English at first. *"Mo athair... An bhfuil mo athair –?"*

"Conor," Eilwen said, taking his hand. It was warm – a stark contrast to the cool, silver night.

Molly *maowed* loudly and trotted to his side. His eyes fluttered and his head rocked. He grimaced, lifting his free hand.

"...*Cá –?*" he began weakly.

He fell silent.

"Conor," Eilwen repeated.

"Cá bhfuil –?"

"Conor, I can't understand you," Eilwen chuckled.

Conor shook his head, then his eyes flew open.

He sat up groggily and swayed. *"Iarann…"* he slurred. Then suddenly his eyes widened, and he began rambling frantically, *"Bhí sé iarann! Cá bhfuil an nathair? An bhfuil sí sábháilte? Cá bhfuil –? Cá bhfuil…* Eilwen!" He exclaimed her name as his eyes fell on her.

Eilwen was smiling ear-to-ear.

Conor returned the smile unsurely. "Where is Gracie?"

"She's all right. She's fine." Without the slightest hesitation, Eilwen lunged forward, throwing her arms around Conor and hugging him as tight as she could. "Thank you," she whispered, for her voice was cracking. Her eyes burned with joy. "Oh, Conor, I'm so… I can't… You saved her!"

She felt Conor's arms slide around her and her stomach flipped. She could not tell if it was his heart or her own that she heard pounding in her ears.

* * *

Conor devoured the food Ygraine had prepared for him. Even after two bowls of stew, three buttered rolls and half a tureen of vegetables, he still finished off a jar of peach preserves and continued popping blackberries into his mouth the entire time he sat on the floor by the fire with Eilwen, trying to teach her to speak Irish.

"Tá sméara dubha agam." She repeated slowly what he had enunciated for her.

"It means, 'I have blackberries,'" Conor said. "Or, 'Blackberries are at me.' There is no verb for having in the Irish. You never *have* a thing. A thing is *at* you. If ya say, 'I have a snake,' it'd be, *Tá nathair agam.* 'A snake is at me.'"

"That makes it sound like a snake's attacking me."

"It doesn't sound so to an Irish-speaker." He popped another blackberry. "How's your shoulder, now?"

Conor was groggy the rest of the night, but not tired enough to sleep. When Ygraine fussed at him to leave Eilwen alone and let her rest, Eilwen protested, insisting she didn't mind. Ygraine relented uncharacteristically and, kissing Conor goodnight, dimmed the fire and went to bed.

Conor immediately asked Eilwen if she wanted to build a blanket fort.

They gathered all the quilts and blankets they could find and, over the course of an hour, constructed a fort whose opening faced the fireplace. "Is Dristan's aunt riled about the pitcher?" Conor asked contritely while tying one corner of the roof to an upturned stool.

"I don't think so." Eilwen tried to sound comforting. "The pitcher did fall apart again, though."

"I figured it would," he mumbled. "What about Dristan? *Maime* says she's going to go and talk to him herself tomorrow."

"Did you drop the pitcher on purpose?" Eilwen asked instead of answering, hiding a smile.

"Of course I didn't!" he snapped. "Well, maybe. I don't think I did. If I did it on purpose, I didn't mean to."

"That doesn't make any sense."

Conor blushed and changed the subject. Eilwen continued smiling to herself, thinking she didn't need to be able to see his aura right now, and feeling a joy she never imagined she'd be lucky enough to feel.

She'd never in her life had as much fun as she did that night. Conor had the peculiar effect of both energizing her and putting her completely at ease. Though she'd always been lonely, Eilwen had also dreaded socializing; even Dristan, whose company she enjoyed, drained her. But Conor didn't. His presence recharged her every bit as much as solitude did.

She never needed to act with Conor. Never felt compelled to hide; to fret over every word for fear of misspeaking; to analyze what she was probably doing wrong. She and Conor talked and giggled and sneaked about all night, sharing stories, adding to the fort, venturing outside to sit in the moonlight and listen to owls... They sat by the fire and read to each other from the books on the shelves; Conor read aloud from a book in Irish while Eilwen followed along on the pages (struggling at first, but her quick ear catching on). They made blackberry tea, and tried to work together to make cookies; Conor began a game where he would instruct Eilwen in Irish, and any time she failed to discern what he meant, she had to spin around three times, or tell Conor something she liked about him, or some other silly thing he thought of.

A few hours before dawn, Eilwen finally began growing sleepy, and curled up in the blankets on the floor of the fort. Conor impishly tried to keep her from slumbering, begging her to keep her eyes open, or constantly asking "Still awake?" or "Are ya listening?" whenever she failed to regularly acknowledge his rambling. When Eilwen finally snapped at him, he quieted and sat at her side, staring at the fire. Eilwen drifted quickly to sleep, unable to remember the last time she'd felt so content.

Though Conor woke her again for breakfast only five hours later, she had never felt so rested.

After breakfast, Eilwen, Conor and Ygraine prepared to venture to complete the tasks left unfinished yesterday. Eilwen stood before a mirror by the door, studying the Eilwen that stared back at her. The clothes Ygraine had given her were loose and cloak-like, the dark blue setting off her yellow eyes. She still wore her own pants and boots, but the upper garments made her look an entirely different person from the orphaned tobacco farmer she was used to seeing in mirrors.

She looked wild. Ancient. Like someone she could imagine running through an enchanted forest. She wondered what Hal would think if he saw her. She did not remove the new clothes, but slipped her coat on over them and placed his cap firmly on her head.

They did not leave until afternoon. Eilwen made herself leave Gracie behind, both for practice being apart as well as for her safety. It was much harder than she anticipated: she kept wanting to go back and check on her "one last time", but eventually Conor and Ygraine coaxed her forward. When they exited the Border and reached the edge of the woods, Ygraine rode Constance to the Duvall cottage, trusting the horse to know the way. "There's iron on the porch, *Mhaime*," Conor warned his mother as she rode off. He and Eilwen were then alone together beneath the oak tree under which they'd met.

"I wonder if Dristan skipped school again today," Eilwen said. "Hope he's okay."

"Where's your room?" Conor asked brusquely.

Eilwen led him to the cabin cautiously. The Ford pickup was not in the drive, so Gus and Mona weren't yet home, but Uncle Dale could be anywhere. She and Conor entered the kitchen from the side porch. "Will your mom be all right?" Eilwen whispered as she led Conor up the stairs to her room.

Conor was not expecting the stairs to be so steep and narrow; he tripped several times, cursing under his breath. "She will. She's intuitive. *Terrifyingly.* If she'd been with us yesterday, she'd have known right off Thelma was fetchin' her dagger."

"But can't you see auras same as her?"

"I can, but *Maime* knows how to interpret what she sees better than I. Comes with experience, I expect. It smells old up here. Goddess, you have this whole upstairs to yourself, then?" Conor stared around the old slave quarters.

"No," said Eilwen. "I share it with Gus."

"But there's only one bed."

"Mine's in the other corner." Eilwen walked over to her straw pile and began digging around beneath her pillow.

"Oh, I, uh… And here I felt bad you had to sleep on the sofa the other night," Conor chuckled awkwardly. He peered over Eilwen's shoulder. "What is it you're lookin' for? You're not wanting to bring your bed, are ya? I can get ya new straw, Eilwen. I understand being sentimental to an *extent*, but —"

Eilwen produced the peanut butter can she kept under her pillow and Conor grew quiet. She was about to open it, then remembered her promise to Old Hal.

As much as she trusted Conor, she'd kept the watch secret for four years – ever since Hal had given it to her. She couldn't break that now. It was her and Hal's secret. She considered stuffing the entire can in her pocket, but knew it wouldn't fit. "Conor, can you go downstairs and stand out front, to make sure Aunt doesn't sneak in?"

Conor nodded and moved carefully down the stairs. Eilwen called softly after him, "Don't step on the stepping stones!"

Alone in the dark, empty room, Eilwen opened the can and removed Hal's pocket watch, the large *H* engraved on the hunter-case gleaming in the faint afternoon light of the dusty windowpanes. She placed the arrowhead and tin soldier in one pocket, the watch in the other. She took a long, sweeping look about the room, feeling oddly sentimental.

After some time, she heard the side door open and realized Conor must have come to warn her of something. She sighed and made her way speedily downstairs, freezing when she saw Uncle Dale slumped at the kitchen table.

She stiffened, not breathing.

She had been fairly quiet. Perhaps Dale hadn't noticed her yet. Could she make it to the exit? If she was silent enough...

Biting her lip, Eilwen moved. She had tiptoed two feet when Dale said, quietly, "I won't tell your aunt."

He said nothing more.

Eilwen froze, face hot. Her uncle's words sank in. Steadily, confusedly, she allowed herself to relax.

She glanced at the door, then back at the man at the table. What little relief she'd gained from his words vanished when she realized that she cared about what was bothering him. He looked lonely. More than that: openly depressed. Eilwen could never remember Uncle Dale emoting in any way that was not in direct response to Aunt's temper. About a minute passed before she found the courage to ask, in a small voice, "What's the matter?"

"Pop's birthday is in three weeks." Dale's voice was unreadable. In front of his hands sat a mug whose contents smelled alcoholic. "And the harvest's about to start. This was his time of year."

Eilwen's stomach felt heavy. Was this what Uncle Dale did all day when everyone was at school? When he had the farm to himself? Did he sit and think sad things like this? Eilwen realized that she had never once considered Dale's feelings in regards to Hal's passing. Eilwen had never even thought of Hal in terms of being Dale's father. Hal had always just been Eilwen's granduncle. Nothing more.

She swallowed, trying to think of something to say. Something to lessen the discomfort in the room.

Dale spoke first. "Was never even able to find that damned watch." His voice was gruff; it tapered into distress before he cleared his throat and spoke evenly. "Haven't seen it in almost five years. I shouldn't worry, 'cause it's been lost longer than this before." His tone betrayed that he had clearly failed to convince himself not to worry. "Pop told me it'd been gone from the family forty years once before it magically showed back up again. He always joked about being lucky, but I reckon he really was just plain old lucky to have that happen to him. Either that, or the watch just wanted damn bad to find him again." He took a swig of his drink. "Here's hoping it wants to find me next. And that it won't take forty years."

He stared out the kitchen window. The only noise was the steady ticking of the grandfather clock in the front hall. Eilwen quietly left the room.

She went through the front door and hopped off the edge of the porch to avoid Hal's gravestone. Conor was sitting in the shady, stone-lined ditch at the end of the yard, red hair popping against the green lily leaves.

Eilwen sat beside him on one of the steps. "This is where I was planning on letting Gracie live before I knew what she was." She moved down into the ditch and motioned Conor do the same. They lay on their stomachs on the cool stone, hidden from the world.

"You said you'd heard horror stories of what happens to witches who find out what they are too late," Eilwen said, the comment seeming come out of nowhere to Conor, who turned his head. "And last night," she continued voicelessly, "your mother told me some witches kill themselves if they don't find out."

Conor was silent a moment. "That's true," he said quietly.

Eilwen stared at the stone steps that faced her. How close had she been, she wondered, to veering down that path? To going mad, or giving up? If Conor hadn't found her two nights ago... would he ever have? It had been luck – sheer luck – that saved her that night.

What if she hadn't been lucky? Why *had* she been lucky? What made her more deserving of answers than any other suffering, lonely, struggling child who can't change no matter how hard she tries?

That was why she needed to save Dristan.

That was why she had to find out if Gus needed saving as well.

Eilwen removed her coat and used it as a pillow against the hard stone while she and Conor waited.

* * *

The Ford pickup rumbled down Bloomfield Road and up the drive. Eilwen covered her nose as exhaust swept over the ditch.

"Catch him before he goes inside," Conor whispered when they heard Gus and Mona walk toward the house, but Eilwen shook her head. "He'll be back out in a bit."

And he was. Some time later, the front door opened and Eilwen heard Gus leap off the porch and patter to the side of the house. She paused to be sure she could not hear Mona, then grabbed her coat. "Stay here," she told Conor. "I'll get him to come to you."

Eilwen stepped out of the ditch and sneaked toward the corner of the house where up against the porch grew Gus's beloved hydrangea. Gus sat as far into the leafy boughs as he could, cross-legged and holding a book. Eilwen could barely hear him mouthing to himself as he read, "*Last night, the moon had a golden ring. And to-night no moon we see!*" He was repeating this a third time when she waved a hand in front of him.

His head jerked up. "Eilwen!"

"Shhh!"

"Sorry!" Gus whispered. Eilwen placed her coat above his head on the porch and sat on the ground, facing him. "Where've you been? What all happened? Are you okay?"

199

"I'm fine. I've been... in the woods."

"For two days?" He paused. "What are you wearing?"

"*Wreck of the Hesperus*?" Eilwen asked, nodding at the book.

"We have to memorize it for tomorrow. You can sit here and learn it with me if ya want."

Eilwen smiled sadly; not just anyone was invited to join Gus under his hydrangea. Nostalgia washed over her – memories, good and bad. "I know it," she said softly. "Hal read it to me once. *Come hither, come hither, my little daughter, and do not tremble so. For I can weather the roughest gale that ever wind did blow.*"

"You remember all that from one hearing?" Gus shook his head in awe. "I dunno how you do that."

Eilwen simply looked at Gus – watched his blue eyes twinkle in the shade. "There's someone I want you to meet." She stood. "But you can't tell Aunt, all right?"

Gus gave her a strange look, but followed her as she led him to the ditch.

"Did you ever find that snake?" he asked as she led him down one of the short flights of stairs.

"Well, yes... But the snake's not who I want you to see."

Gus gasped quietly when he saw Conor. He took a few steps back. Eilwen gently told him, "It's okay," and beckoned him down.

Conor, who seemed uncertain as well, glanced over Gus's person, but Eilwen then saw his uncertainty dissolve, transitioning into the sweet but awkwardly-restrained enthusiasm that defined him so. Gus was nervous, but Conor smiled warmly at the ten-year-old and radiated encouragement. "So you're August Henry, are ya?"

"Gus," the boy said, now less uneasy.

"Gus, then."

"Are you one of Eilwen's friends?" Gus asked.

"I am."

"I ain't seen you at school before."

"Well, I'm not exactly enrolled."

"Who are you, then?"

Conor looked unsure. Before he could respond, Eilwen spoke: "Gus, you remember Gracie?" Conor looked confusedly at Eilwen. "The fairy doll Old Hal gave me when you were real little," Eilwen clarified. "The one he bought at that store in town?"

"The one Aunt threw in the fire?" Gus asked, sounding apologetic as soon as he said this.

Eilwen nodded while Conor snorted, "As though fire could hurt a fairy."

Gus gave Conor an odd look. Eilwen said, "You remember all those stories Old Hal used to tell us, too. Right Gus? About fairies, and magic?"

"Yeah, but they were just stories after all," said Gus slowly. He transferred his odd look to Eilwen. "What are you on about? I ain't being pranked, am I?"

"No, no, not at all! Gus, I just… I was worried…" She sighed. "Conor, can you tell anything? Anything at all?"

Conor, who appeared to be studying Gus's aura intently, glanced briefly at Eilwen, and in that glance Eilwen discerned a definite and unequivocal *no*.

Her shoulders fell. If she was honest with herself she would admit she was not surprised. But she was disappointed. "Gus, you never believed any of those stories of Hal's? Never even played pretend they could be real?"

"Nah, never. I only like to play pretend I'm a war hero, or a soldier. Something real, like that," said Gus. "Sometimes Thomas and me play pretend we're off fighting Germans like Uncle used to. That's the kind of pretending I do. The other stuff's nonsense."

Eilwen was quietly aghast. How could her little brother – her own flesh and blood – be so unlike her? Be so unlike Hal?

Was she really surprised, though? She couldn't tell. She couldn't be surprised at the confirmation of what she'd known all these years: that she and her brother were different. Or was it simply that this was the first stark difference between herself and her brother she'd observed that was not skin deep, or marriage-certificate related?

Suddenly the front door burst open. Eilwen gasped and ducked down. She reached up to pull Gus down as well, but it was too late: they'd been spotted.

"August Henry, is that your no-account sister hidin' in those ditch lilies?" Mona demanded.

Her staccato footsteps pierced the earth as she hurried toward the ditch.

"Conor, make yourself invisible!" Eilwen hissed to Conor, who had ducked beside her. He tried frantically to mumble the words for the spell but was too frightened: his image warbled, but he could not seem to make himself vanish. The blood drained from Eilwen's face.

Gus appeared too confused to fully comprehend what Eilwen had just ordered Conor to do. Instead he relented and stood right as Mona reached the edge of the ditch.

"She ain't hurting nothing," was his simple response.

Mona obviously didn't care in the slightest. "Eilwen Tabb, you get your lazy ass up here and get started on all those chores you left for us to take care of while you were off doing God knows what with… with… and just who in God's name is *this?*" She gestured violently toward Conor with her free hand. With her other, she held the coat that Eilwen had left on the porch.

What little blood remained in Eilwen's face drained as well.

She stood straight up. "Yes ma'am, I'll get right –"

"No!" Conor stood beside Eilwen, glaring at Mona. "She doesn't have to listen to you anymore!"

Eilwen whimpered in panic, trying to make Conor hush.

"You watch your mouth, boy." Mona was so un-intimidated that she appeared almost amused. "Heaven and Earth, Eilwen, how'd you find yourself *another* piece of Irish trash this fast?"

Conor growled as he clambered out of the ditch –

"Gwydion Conor!"

Ygraine's voice carried from Bloomfield Road, where she could be seen walking briskly toward the Homestead.

Mona's head whipped toward the voice. She said nothing, face terrifyingly stern, but studied the red-haired witch that approached as a hawk studies a potential catch before determining when and how to attack: cautious, alert… yet completely and utterly unimpressed.

"D'ya hear what she called me, though, *Mhaime!*" Conor called back, as Ygraine hurried up the drive.

"I'll call ya far worse if you lay one finger on a defenseless mundane!" Ygraine snapped. "And on her own land, of all places!"

"And just who the Hell are you?" demanded Mona, as Ygraine reached the lily ditch. "Is this redheaded rat yours?"

"My *son*, Conor," Ygraine introduced with alarming calmness. She reached her son's side and placed a restraining hand on his shoulder (Conor looked livid enough to spontaneously combust). "I take it this charming young man," she nodded toward a panic-stricken Gus, "belongs to you?"

"My *nephew*," Mona seethed. "And that yellow-eyed heathen is my niece. Would you care to tell me where she's been?"

Ygraine gave an uncharacteristic pause of confusion, staring at and about Mona a second or two longer than was usual for her to do when reading auras.

"With me," she responded finally.

"And just who are you?" Mona demanded again.

Eilwen was eyeing the coat in Mona's hand with her life. Why – oh why – had she left it on the porch? Left her precious gifts from Hal in its pockets? Could she grab it and run? Could she be that brave?

Ygraine and Mona were face to face, neither flinching, neither backing down, both arguing; shortly and curtly at first, over what was to be done about Eilwen and the matter of her residency. But the exchange grew savage, at least on the part of Mona. Even Ygraine, despite

204

maintaining a comparatively even temperament, appeared shocked at the senseless vehemence with which Mrs. Hittle armed herself. Eilwen, Conor and Gus cowered on the sidelines, each as confused and terrified as the other, each for different reasons.

Finally Mona threw the coat into the ditch in a screaming rage. Eilwen leapt at it, as a starved animal leaps at a crumb, and gathered it into her arms, feeling life and warmth return to her body.

"TAKE HER, THEN!" Spittle flew from Mona's mouth; her body shook, her flagrant rage met only by the still silence of the surrounding neutral farmstead – a soundless afternoon. Not a leaf stirred. "Take her and get her off my hands! Just one less God damned mouth to feed! I've wanted to get rid of her since she got here anyhow! Just take her and DON'T COME BACK!"

Mona stormed into the house. A moment later, she threw the front door open again and screamed for Gus to come in after her. Not daring to even consider disobeying, Gus mouthed his usual *I'm sorry* to Eilwen, his words – even voicelessly – heavy with reluctance and guilt. Then, with eyes glistening, Eilwen's little brother hurried into the house after their aunt. The front door did not slam shut, but the sound nonetheless carried as though louder than a gunshot to Eilwen's ears.

She paled, eyes stinging, chest barely moving.

What had just happened? What words had been exchanged? Had Eilwen heard them correctly? Or had they been said at all? Or had they indeed been said, and were simply too glorious – too unimaginably wonderful – for Eilwen's browbeaten soul to accept as real?

Was Eilwen free?

"*Mhaime?*" Conor looked up at his mother.

"We're leaving," Ygraine replied curtly, staring in angered disbelief after where Mona had disappeared. Then, reassuringly calm, she added, "Come now, Eilwen, we're taking ya home."

Ygraine began walking. Eilwen, trembling, hurried alongside Conor to keep up with his mother's quick strides.

"I spoke with Dristan and his aunt," Ygraine explained as they neared the side of the house, Eilwen still struggling to keep calm. "He'll be takin' some time to 'take it all in', as he said. His aunt as well. I'll come back and fetch him to spend a weekend with us a few weeks from now, when he feels more settled with the idea."

Eilwen merely nodded, guiltily realizing she'd completely forgotten about Dristan. She looked at Conor and noticed his head was covered with straw. "Conor," she began, then realized she was covered in straw as well. So was Ygraine.

They looked up to see handful upon handful of straw being thrown from a window of Eilwen and Gus's room. Eilwen felt relief mix with absolute panic inside her as she realized how miraculously lucky she was that she'd procured Hal's gifts beforehand. The thought that Mona had been this close – *this close* – to literally uncovering Eilwen's hiding place for them – where they had resided for years only up until this very afternoon – made her legs and body tremble all the more.

Mona was tossing out Eilwen's bed.

When she finished, she leaned out the window, face red as ever. "UNGRATEFUL BASTARD!" she screeched. "Just like your mother! Whoring and running around with whatever drunken wanderin' newcomer catches her eye!"

Tears threatened in Eilwen's eyes. She had lost her home and family, terrible though they were. Should she feel happy or sad? She didn't know what to feel. Part of her was still afraid to allow herself to feel anything: she choked trying to fight back a sob, but her efforts failed. Weak from grief and conflict, she let herself cry, despite how weary she was from crying already; her eyes were sore, her chest ached. But the urge to cry stopped short.

Conor had taken her hand in his, and was squeezing it tightly.

Eilwen did not flinch at all.

Chapter X

The Uktena Child

Here Roundhead, the warrior, came Prophet to meet,
Saying, "If you're from Heaven I'll kneel at your feet";
But our chiefs again the illusions dispel
Pronouncing the Prophet the agent of hell.
– Anonymous, "The Shawnees at Wapakoneta"

The fact that Gracie grew in size over the next few weeks eased Eilwen's concerns regarding her age; though Gracie lacked juvenile markings, she was clearly not finished growing.

Life at the Sheehan cottage was such sweet refuge that Eilwen went to bed each night and woke each morning terrified she was dreaming. Gradually though, she began to feel safe: this was real. And it would be an affront to Conor and Ygraine – who had given her this new life and asked nothing in return – to not allow herself to enjoy it. She grew happy over the last week of August and first week of September. She laughed with Conor, and enjoyed Ayasta and Ivy's visits. She ate heartily, slept deeply, and eventually felt her panic-conditioned mind relax and accept that the threat of the switch no longer governed her. She was free. For the first time in her life, Eilwen Tabb was free – free to laugh at what tickled her, to voice her thoughts, to feel and not be punished.

Eilwen had free time as well. The tiny Sheehan farm did not require nearly so much labor as the Hittles': she helped Conor tend the animals in the mornings and evenings, gather eggs from the henhouse, and harvest whatever berries and vegetables where ripe, but aside from that she had no obligations. Her day was a blank slate. Unused to this freedom, she felt herself panicking once the initial joy of endless daydreaming faded. She was used to thinking that if she was doing nothing, she was slacking off. Conor kept her busy by teaching her Irish and what magic he could; he mostly helped her strengthen her connection to the Fire element. "Your connection to Earth is alarmingly strong for an Air witch," he observed one day, when Eilwen sniffed a patch of soil and instantly knew it was not the right dirt for the plants he'd been trying to grow in it. "Earth is Air's opposite. Earth should be the one you struggle with." But Eilwen loved Earth. It came to her almost as easily as Air. It comforted her. It was stable.

Eilwen spent most of her time going on walks with Gracie. She would wander the forests on the Border's edge, following game trails or creeks for hours on end, her snake slithering beside her or racing along branches from tree to tree. They found hideaways in hollow trunks, grottos, and limestone caves dripping with moss and fungi. Eilwen would sit in these places and read books from Ygraine's shelves while Gracie hunted, climbed or swam. She and Gracie had picnics whenever Eilwen slipped bread and fruits from the kitchen and eggs from the henhouse in her coat pockets. (One day she tripped and cracked an egg in her pocket, and had to rinse out her coat in a brook while Gracie grouchily slithered off to find something else to eat.) Some afternoons Eilwen would find a mossy spot and nap, reveling in the silent solitude and wet stillness of the forest air. Gracie slept with her, either coiled on her stomach or curled around her neck.

The only thing missing was the tobacco harvest.

On September thirteenth, Conor found her alone in the animal barn, up on one of the rafters. "You seem sad of late," he said.

"Today is Hal's birthday," Eilwen responded distantly.

"Is it, now?" Conor climbed a little ways up a nearby rafter. "That explains it, then."

"Explains what?"

"Your draw to Earth. Your granduncle was a Virgo, wasn't he? Even if he weren't a warlock, he'd still've had an Earthly affinity. Your connection to him gives ya your strong tie to Earth."

Eilwen was suddenly blinking away tears.

Conor said, "I'm going to touch ya now, Eilwen," and tugged gently on her sleeve. "Come on down. Feel like takin' a trip?"

When Eilwen asked him where he was taking her, he said it was a surprise. However, after he and Eilwen had dressed for travel, tacked one of the horses and ridden out of the Border, he realized aloud that it couldn't be a surprise after all because he didn't know the way. "Which way to town?"

After about an hour of plodding through countryside, they were clopping down Boston Road in downtown Bardstown. Automobiles chuckled and horses drew carts and wagons up and down the streets. The air was less chilly here and carried a very different tapestry of sounds and smells than the country. Eilwen had to concentrate to keep from growing over-stimulated: this was her first time in town since her senses had heightened.

Conor was soon lost, having walked them clear to the other side of town. "Where'd your uncle buy you that doll?" he asked. Eilwen directed him back past St. Joseph's cathedral and took the reins the rest of the way.

They tethered the horse outside the toy shop, the cloak-like coats they wore against the autumn chill concealing their anachronistic clothes. The storeowner greeted them as they stepped inside and watched in amusement as Conor darted around, looking at books, toys and knickknacks. Finally, the warlock found the shelves with the dolls and told Eilwen to pick one she liked.

"Do you have money?" Eilwen asked in surprise.

"*Maime* keeps mundane money for travel emergencies. We haven't traveled in ages, though. Go on, pick one."

Eilwen selected the doll most similar in appearance she could find to her old one, but nearly fainted when she saw the price. "Conor, it's two *whole dollars!*" God in Heaven, was this what Hal had spent on her the day he'd bought Gracie?

Conor shrugged. "This the one you want? Answer truthful, now, I'll know if you're lying." Eilwen guiltily nodded. Conor smiled and got in line at the counter.

They waited while the woman in front of them helped the storeowner tally the prices of the children's books she was buying. Meanwhile Eilwen held her doll, tracing the primped waves of hair around the pale face. Like all the other dolls, its skin was pink, porcelain white. Not a hint of tan. Not the slightest browning. "Conor," she asked absently, "when we were talking to Aunt and Gus a few weeks back, and Aunt told you I was her niece…" She hesitated, realizing she was afraid of the answer no matter what it was. "…Was she lying?"

Conor paused. "You suspect you're not really her niece?"

Eilwen nodded, then shook her head, then shrugged. "I don't know. I've wondered sometimes."

"I suspected as much. Mother did as well. She even thought you might be… Never the matter. No, darlin', your aunt weren't lying."

Eilwen was not prepared for the disappointment that washed over her. "She wasn't?"

"Afraid not." Conor looked ready to say more, but sighed and rolled his eyes when the woman in front of them suddenly declared she'd lost count of her money and needed to start over.

"But you said you're not as good at interpreting auras as your mother," Eilwen protested. "Maybe you could've misread —"

"There's no interpretation needed in telling if a body's lying or not," Conor explained gently, lowering his voice. "There's a telltale shift in the aura when a person fabricates to avoid the truth. Skillful interpretation is needed to tell *why* a person's lying, but simply telling if they're lying or not? No skill needed. Liars give themselves away. All Fires do is notice."

"So Aunt Mona wasn't lying," Eilwen summarized dejectedly.

Conor shook his head. "You're every bit as much her niece as August Henry is her nephew. She was tellin' the full truth of it."

The woman in front of them finished paying and hurried out of the shop. Conor muttered "About time," and stepped up to the counter.

* * *

The day of the equinox, Eilwen was a nervous wreck. "They won't like me. People never like me. I always mess things up."

"I like you," said Conor quietly. He was sitting on his bed reading a book of Welsh fairytales while Eilwen paced around his loft.

"You're different, though," she said. "You're not people. You're Conor. You're special."

Conor lowered his face and blushed. Eilwen stood at his diamond-paned window, staring at the tree line across the glade: a sea of red and yellow against a blue sky. "What if they don't accept me? Will I still get to live with you, in the Border, at least? I can't go back to the Homestead!"

"If *Maime* didn't think they'd accept you, she wouldn't introduce ya in the first of it. And they'll be doing nothing to irk her. They'll do anything to persuade her to rejoin and no mistake."

"Why did she leave the coven again?" Eilwen inquired, remembering how Conor had avoided the question last the time she'd asked.

He did the same now: the normally loquacious and voluntarily informative Conor replied simply, curtly, "Political differences."

Eilwen pressed no further.

That evening, she and Conor began preparing to leave for the coven. While doing so, Conor said to her, unprompted and without any preamble, "Anything you might hear tonight – anything not related to your induction – ignore it. All right? Nothing… nothing's written in stone." He was brisk but emphatic. Eilwen, confused and now even more worried, just nodded.

On the back edge of the Sheehans' glade there opened into the trees a wide trail. Eilwen, Conor and Ygraine began on it before dusk. As they walked, Eilwen realized she was growing excited – *excited*, not just worried. Amid the silence of the ancient trees there emerged the signs of civilization: mooing cattle and bleating goats, followed by the more intimate noises of hinges creaking and the tinkling of wind chimes. The smells of burning wood and smoked food mixed with the sugary scent of fallen leaves. Eilwen realized, as she, Conor and Ygraine drew nearer the end of the trail, that they were approaching another break in the trees – the vastest glade she'd ever seen, such that she could barely see the forest begin again on the other side. Conor leapt ahead and said, "Welcome to New Salem!" He stepped out of the trees and followed the trail into the sleepy, antiquated village that seemed to have appeared out of nowhere.

The hilly land was scattered with trees, cabins, and barns. Split-rail fences rose and fell with the half-shaded terrain, separating sheep, goats and pigs, while horses and cows grazed lazily. In the distance were acres of wheat, corn, sunflowers, flax and hay. Eilwen's eye was instinctively drawn to three empty fields which a powerful feeling told her had recently been home to tobacco.

She hurried to catch up to Conor. Ygraine, who had hardly breathed a word, walked patiently behind.

"Ivy lives over there," Conor said when Eilwen reached him, waving toward the west of the village. "Spends a lot of time with the Cherokee coven, so she mightn't be home. The Alders have belonged to both covens since the Revolution. Jonathon Alder was captured by Shawnees as a boy. His daughter's line has lived within the Border since the time of Tecumseh, whose brother became obsessed with witch-hunting. The Alder witches no longer felt safe with the Shawnee, so the Cherokee witches invited them into the Border. They knew they had to stick together, what with their magic being demonized and their *pawakas* being destroyed."

"*Pawakas*?" asked Eilwen, as Conor led her to a sleeping fire pit in the center of the village. It was surrounded by regal-looking cabins with clusters of oaks, ashes and hawthorns in between – the only order apparent in the entire layout of the village.

"Spirit pouches," Conor said, as though Eilwen were expected to understand. "Smaller, personal versions of Sacred Bundles. Tenskwatawa the witch hunter had almost all the original Bundles destroyed over a hundred years ago. Only a handful remain."

"What's a Sacred Bundle?"

"Ancient magic. Terribly powerful. And dangerous because. Only one witch in a generation is trained to work with her coven's Bundle. It's her life's duty. She alone is able to consult it. And only on special occasions, the solstices, and in dire emergencies. A Sacred Bundle was used in the creation of the Border. It's why its protective magic is so powerful."

"Why'd the witch hunter hate the Bundles so much? Wasn't he Shawnee himself?"

"Aye, but a traitorous rat of one," said Conor. His voice grew dark. "He turned on his own people. His aim was to purify his race, the same way Catholics tried to purify pagans: killing off old believers, contorting legends, winning over the weak-minded with lies of how the old ways are similar to the new. That's why Catholics worship Mary, ya see. They won over Irish pagans – my own kind – with bullshite stories of Mary bein' the Goddess."

"You're pagan?" was all Eilwen got out of that.

Conor gave her an odd look. "What'd ya think I was?"

"Is it possible for a witch to still be Christian?"

"Of course. I hate the ruddy blighter, but look at Dristan: his mam was a witch *and* a devout, church-goin' Catholic all her life, apparently."

"Yeah, but Catholics aren't Christian. Also, why do you hate Dristan so much?"

Eilwen never got her answer: a small crowd had begun to gather around the fire pit and Conor said they needed to find a seat. He led her to a spot on the ground upfront. They sat together as the crowd thickened and the sky darkened.

"Where's Ygraine?" Eilwen asked.

"Likely talking with Arden, the High Priestess. She'll be the one deciding whether to admit you."

Eilwen swallowed. Conor gave his usual warning before taking her hand. Her stomach flipped when she felt him tenderly stroke her fingers with his thumb.

The fire pit burst into life: yellow flames licked the purple sky. Already the embers glowed as though they'd

216

been burning for hours. Eilwen gazed around at the people, some – mostly children – sitting up front as she and Conor were. Most stood, some holding children in their arms or on shoulders. Their many faces were lively and brilliant, the firelight exacerbating the glow that seemed natural to the countless eyes that ranged from yellow, brown, green to blue of every shade. Eilwen did a double-take when she spied a pair of negro sisters, one with yellow eyes and one with eyes as green as emeralds, sitting across the fire from her. Two black girls, she thought incredulously. Sitting up front. With white folk sitting around them as though it were the most normal thing in the world. Eilwen thought back bitterly on all the times Mona had threatened to pass her off as a darkie just as an excuse to make Eilwen have to sit away from the rest of the family in public.

Silence fell and an elegantly dressed woman with auburn hair appeared in the center of the circle. Arden MacNessa, High Priestess of New Salem, was a presence as intimidating as Ygraine Sheehan if only for the fact that one could feel through intuition alone this woman was looking at more than your face or posture – one felt that somehow Arden's eyes were on them even if she were merely standing nearby and looking another direction. Eilwen could tell she was Fire before Conor told her.

Her Familiar was a rattlesnake.

The rest of the coven's council was composed of four witches, one representative of each element: an Air witch named Finola; a Water named Múireann; an Earth named Siobnan; and another Fire, named Reagan. Reagan entered the circle and her eyes fell swiftly upon Conor and then rested on Eilwen, who shifted and moved closer to him.

Ygraine entered the circle last. She strode to where Arden and her council stood, but gave them only formal acknowledgment and made it quite apparent she was distancing herself.

"Political differences?" Eilwen whispered to Conor.

Conor stared into the fire and nodded.

The four witches of the Council dispersed to stand in a circle around the fire, equidistant from one another. Arden remained where she stood. "We have a visitor tonight," was her statement of greeting.

Eilwen suddenly felt the eyes in the crowd fall on her. Her face grew hot. Conor tightened his hold on her hand but that only made it worse.

"Eilwen Margaret Tabb," Arden continued. Her deep purple robes made her hair and eyes seem the color of rubies. "I bid you stand, young tobacco farmer."

Eilwen felt frozen: she had not been expecting anything so public. She stared, dumbstruck and afraid, at Arden for several seconds before Conor whispered, "Get up, Eilwen." She hesitated. He squeezed her hand and nudged her. "Up. Now."

Eilwen scrambled gracelessly to her feet.

"Eilwen is a witch rescued, and currently holds the honor of residing with our very own Ygraine Sheehan, and her son Gwydion Conor. Ygraine herself tells me Eilwen is powerful, ripe with potential, and that she seeks to join our coven. Tell me, child," she addressed Eilwen directly, "what is your element?"

"Air," Eilwen stated with voiceless timidity, then cleared her throat and repeated the word slightly louder.

"And where is your Familiar?"

"As the girl has been in my charge, I have been schooling her in the practice of prolonged separation from her Familiar," Ygraine answered for Eilwen. "Just as I do my son. All our animals are at home."

Arden seemed understanding. "Tell us, then, Eilwen, what your Familiar *is*."

Eilwen looked at Ygraine, who nodded. "A black racer, ma'am."

"A snake!" cried someone in the crowd. There was a subsequent bout of murmuring and Eilwen felt the eyes fixed upon her widen – felt their gazes intensify. She wished she could sit.

Arden was the only witch who appeared unalarmed; Eilwen suspected Ygraine had briefed her beforehand, and that this public interview was merely for the sake of the coven. "Potentially powerful indeed," was how Arden silenced the crowd.

"There is another witchling who lives not far from where Eilwen was raised," Ygraine announced when the whisperings subsided. "Dristan Joseph McAtee. A Water warlock, not much older than my own son. He seems gifted as well, and will be visitin' us in a week's time. I ask that the Council take my word for his character in his absence, and consider his admittance in your deliberations regarding Eilwen."

"You have my word." Arden bowed her head.

Eilwen was permitted to sit again. Shortly after – once Arden had made a few more announcements that Eilwen, in her dazed and nervous state, unintentionally tuned out – the celebration of the equinox began. Conor smiled proudly at her as they sat together under an oak some ways from the crowded fire pit. Witches and warlocks were dancing around the bonfire to the music of fiddles, drums, flutes and mandolins. The smell of the feast that had been laid out was mouthwatering, and Eilwen and Conor shamelessly gorged themselves. Conor even sneaked a goblet of wine for them to share. "You did well!" he beamed.

Eilwen blushed and smiled. "I wasn't expecting to have to stand in front of everyone."

"Aye, get used to that. You'll be havin' to do it again when you're initiated. And again when ya turn thirteen."

"But I don't know when that is."

"You'll know." Conor seemed certain of this. "It's a magical birthday. Care to dance, would ya?" He held out a hand to her.

Eilwen had never danced before. Yet alone with a boy. She'd never been allowed to attend church picnics or school dances. But next to conjuring the rushing power of wind, dancing with Conor was the most magical moment of her life. She didn't know what she was doing – she was prepared for none of the sudden bounces, twirls or changes in direction. But she felt solidly in her element. Music – organized sound, a harmonic synthesis of vibrations and waves – flowed around them, uplifting them as she and Conor moved with instinctive and unrehearsed synchronization as playfully as wind itself. Eilwen never stopped smiling.

When the song ended, Conor held her close and laughed that he needed to sit. After they sat, he continued clinging to her. "I need somethin' to hold onto. I drank too much," was his transparent excuse, and when Eilwen pointed out that he'd only had a few sips, he just held her tighter. Eilwen, thrilled, argued no more and hugged him back. They sat beneath their oak tree, holding each other, watching the other witches dancing in the firelight.

It felt so odd, Eilwen thought as she relaxed in the warm security of his arms, to let someone hold her like this. To feel the touch of another human and not want to flinch away. She could feel the achingly-restrained intensity of his embrace. When Conor grew bold enough to reach up and stroke her cheek, she felt her heart leap into her throat – felt it *pounding* in her ears. She wondered dizzily if Conor could hear it, for he became encouraged: his face drew nearer. Eilwen thought she would lose her mind when she felt him rub his nose against hers.

He was so warm. So terribly, wonderfully warm.

"Am I interrupting?"

Ivy Alder was suddenly beside them, grinning childishly. Eilwen gasped.

Conor gasped, then spat what sounded like a curse in Irish. "*Damn* it to *Hell*, Ivy!"

Ivy burst out laughing. Conor looked angry enough to steam. "This is bold, Conor. The whole Council's here!"

"Good!" Conor snorted. "Now *go away!*"

"But Asta's with me. She's getting food right now. She sent me over to sit with you."

Conor glared at Ivy as he and Eilwen released each other. Eilwen rested her head on his shoulder. He slid his arm back around her and held her against him.

Her head was spinning. Had Conor really been about to kiss her? This was too magical to be real. She was dreaming. She had to be. Yet she knew she wasn't, and she smiled, replaying in her mind those moments in his arms. The braver part of her tried to imagine how it would have felt to have their lips meet, but knew her imaginings could do it no justice. Holding Conor's hand was a difficult-enough euphoria to replicate in daydreams. She could not possibly imagine kissing him. That was one daydream that *had* to become real.

Eilwen couldn't believe it: she had feelings. For a boy. And he seemed to have feelings for *her*. Realizing this alarmed her almost as much as it had alarmed her to learn she was a witch. Eilwen's life had been devoid of love and magic for so long. But then Conor Sheehan had come along. Conor Sheehan had changed everything.

* * *

Ayasta joined Ivy, Conor and Eilwen with a heaping plate of food, and the four ate and talked under the oak tree. Eilwen was having a wonderful time: Ivy and Asta asked how she was adjusting to her new life, and discussed all the fun things they could do together to make her feel at home ("I'll teach you how to shoot a bow proper," Ivy offered. "Then you can come hunting with us!"). They seemed particularly interested in this Water warlock Ygraine had described, and inquired vigorously about Dristan, which made Conor grumble.

"Is he handsome?" Ayasta asked (Eilwen couldn't help chuckling at how strongly she was reminded of Agnes). "Maybe if he's attractive enough he'll catch Epona's eye and —"

"Asta, don't you have a weasel to enchant?" Conor interrupted rudely.

Ayasta's yellow eyes narrowed on him.

"I just hope he's not a sissy," said Ivy. Eilwen smiled, amused at the thought of this short, scrawny eleven-year-old teaching her how to wield a deadly hunting weapon. Then she rubbed her shoulder. "All the Waters I know are. Asta's sister scraped her knee the other day and cried."

"She's five!" said Ayasta.

A small cheer bubbled briefly from the crowd around the bonfire. Reagan, the Fire priestess, had a young witch by her side and the two seemed to be giving a speech. Eilwen strained to listen but Conor leaned in close: "The village is deserted, what with everyone around the bonfire," he whispered. "How'd you like a private tour of New Salem?"

Eilwen nodded enthusiastically and allowed him to pull her to her feet. Ayasta watched with an expression Eilwen couldn't quite read as Conor bid her and Ivy farewell and whisked Eilwen away from the festivities.

The village was indeed deserted. Calm, quiet night had enveloped the glade, the shapes of homes, trees and fences just discernible against deep blue grass. Owls hooted and crickets chirped. The air was crisp and still. A near-full moon dominated the starry sky while chickens softly clucked and cows shifted sleeping positions. Save for

Eilwen and Conor, meandering hand-in-hand between fields and houses, not a human was in sight.

Eilwen found herself missing Gracie. She felt guilty when she voiced this aloud, for Conor was doing so much to keep her happy, but he was not slighted. "I miss the little racer as well." He paused. "D'ya know the reason the black racer is black?" he asked conversationally. They were passing a horse paddock with a drinking pond near the fence, the moon reflected in the water. Eilwen shook her head as Conor helped her onto the fence and climbed up to sit next to her.

"They say the black racer was one of the animals who tried to bring the gift of fire to the world," he began. "In the beginning, there was no fire. The world was cold. Then the Thunders struck lightning and lit a flame at the bottom of a hollow tree on an island surrounded by water. All the animals knew the fire was there because they could see the smoke, and many tried to bring the fire with them back to the rest of the world. All failed except for the Water Spider. But one of the animals who tried was the *Uksu'hi* – the Black Racer. She swam across the water to the island and entered the tree through a hole near the roots. But the heat and smoke were too much for her, and she darted about over the coals and hot ashes until she was almost on fire herself. She managed to escape, but she was forever scorched black. And to this day she still races about, as though trying to escape close quarters."

"No wonder Gracie didn't like you at first," Eilwen teased. "Fire traumatized her."

"I also saved her life," Conor said with a fake cockiness. He still had her hand in his. "I think that more than makes up for it."

"I'd risk getting scorched if it meant bringing fire back with me," Eilwen heard herself say boldly.

Even in the darkness, Conor's face brightened. He had just opened his mouth to respond when they heard footsteps.

Ayasta appeared suddenly around the corner of a barn. "You're not telling stories without me, are you?"

Eilwen heard Conor groan. She couldn't blame him: this was the second time they'd been interrupted that night. Still, they welcomed Ayasta, and she climbed up onto the fence with them.

"Asta's a stunning storyteller," Conor told Eilwen. "She's studying to be an orator for her tribe. Memorizing all the songs and stories and whatnot."

"Mostly whatnot." Ayasta grinned. "The snake stories are my favorites, though. Telling Eilwen about her racer?"

"You could better than I."

"No, you did fine. For an Irishman."

"And what's that mean?"

Ayasta chuckled. "I just think it's funny to hear a warlock from a land with no snakes telling a witch about *her* snake."

"Well, I'm not exactly *from* Ireland, am I?" Conor snipped, and then looked suddenly sullen, like he'd saddened himself.

Ayasta patted his shoulder.

"Could you tell us another snake story?" Eilwen asked her, hoping to distract Conor from whatever was bothering him. "I noticed Arden had a rattlesnake."

"Rattlers are the most sacred of the snakes," Ayasta explained. "It was a rattlesnake choosing Arden that convinced my people she and the other immigrant witches could be trusted. So we gave them this glade, and they settled it and named it New Salem."

"Immigrant witches?" Eilwen recalled Mona complaining vigorously about immigrants. One of the teachers Mona worked with was married to a tobacco farmer who had hired a small family of German refugees a few years back: they spoke fractured, heavily-accented English and lived in a shack near the fields they were paid to help tend, and were known around the countryside as just "the four Jews." Mona had never met them, but had developed a healthy hatred for them solely because, "It's bad enough I have to see headlines about that damned New Deal on half the magazines I pass in town – why the hell would I want to see fear-mongering nonsense about made-up concentration camps on the other half? It's not as though I'm ever going to Germany."

Were the four Jews magic? Eilwen wondered. Could they be immigrant witches too? Did witches even immigrate for the same reasons mundanes did? Eilwen asked this aloud. "Sometimes," Ayasta nodded. "More often to escape persecution than to fulfill some American Dream. Arden and her coven came over with the mundane immigrants, but then sought safety among native magic people. Arden's mother was the first European witch to seek contact with my coven after we

226

permanently separated ourselves from our own mundanes."

"It seems like witches have to hide from mundanes no matter their culture," Eilwen observed, not hiding her bitterness at the injustice.

Then she felt a spark of glee: she was truly considering herself a witch now, she realized. Part of a group. Part of her own type of people. She felt pride for what she was – pride in belonging. She had something to belong *to* for once in her life.

Assuming Arden lets me join, her worried nature readily reminded her.

"If being a storyteller teaches you anything, it's that every culture has both magic it worships, and magic it hates." Ayasta pulled her knees up to her chin and wrapped her arms around them as she studied the moon's reflection in the pond. "Cherokee witches have had to hide ourselves from Cherokee mundanes just as often Ygraine says the Irish witches hide from theirs. Ygraine hailed from a coven in Ireland that had a protective Border like ours. Only we used Uktena magic in our spell – I'm not sure what the Irish use for spells that strong."

"Their spell's *not* that strong." Conor's sullenness was returning. "It gets damaged. Sometimes fails altogether. My da says no Irish witch or warlock ever gets a sound night's sleep for the fear of it."

"Irish magic has had more centuries being weakened by iron. No American even knew what iron was until you whites brought it over."

"And Iron will destroy this Border one day too," replied Conor. "One day the spells that make intruders get lost in the woods won't work. There'll be enough iron that no spell will. And all the fairies and goblins that protect the forest will be as extinct as the Uktena."

"Wasn't the Uktena killed off by ancient Americans, though?" Eilwen asked.

"It's a complicated story," said Ayasta.

"Can you tell it?"

Ayasta smiled. "I would need to start at the very beginning – *thousands* of years ago."

Eilwen nodded eagerly and scooted closer. Even Conor lifted his head.

"Long ago," Ayasta began, "before the Great Serpents even existed, there was a woman. She was not a favorite in her village: taboo surrounded her, from the superstitious day of her birth to the fact that her parents were unwed, and she grew up to be the petty, unlawful outcast as which she was treated. The Cherokee called her *Uktena*, which meant 'keen-eyed,' because she survived from day-to-day through cunning thievery.

"One day, Uktena had a daughter, and though Uktena raised her to survive as an outcast too, her daughter was tenderhearted and insightful, and saw the injustice of her mother's life. She was welcome in the village for her kind nature, but though the Cherokee forgave her for her heritage, no one relented to her requests to forgive and love her mother as well.

"The Moon and Sun were still young at this time, and often acted childishly. One day, the Sun complained that none of the humans ever smiled at her, and the Moon mocked her for this: 'The humans *adore* me,' bragged the Moon. 'They look up at me and smile each time I cross the sky.' The next day, the Sun, overcome with envy and anger, saw the humans squint and turn away again, and in her ire, sent a heat sickness to kill them all.

"One by one, people and animals dropped dead from the heat. What few remained held a council, and realized the only solution was to kill the Sun. Uktena was told she would be forgiven if she accomplished this, so she agreed, and was transformed into a great snake by the shamans, then told to go to the sky's edge where the Sun lives and kill her. However, the shamans also transformed another human into the first rattlesnake, to help with the task, and the rattlesnake raced ahead of Uktena and reached the Sun's home first. It accidentally killed the sun's daughter by mistake, but when the rattlesnake returned home, it was venerated, for the Sun's grief ended the heat. Uktena, angry and envious, returned home as well, but grew angrier and more hostile over time, so that the Cherokee feared how dangerous she had become.

"Another council was held, and the people decided to banish Uktena to *Galunlati* – the land where the monsters live. Uktena's daughter begged them to reconsider, but the decision was final, and Uktena was forced to leave the mortal world forever. But what the humans did not know was that Uktena had laid eggs throughout the wilderness, and that they would hatch and grow and become the great dragons of Turtle Island. Uktena's daughter was the first guardian of the eggs. She kept them hidden from the other humans, protecting them until they hatched, and then loved and cared for her little sisters.

"It is said that the daughter of Uktena begat the line of royalty that would one day rule the chiefdoms. And that each daughter in that line was charged with protecting the offspring of the dragons – a secret responsibility they guarded with their lives. But even with the queens looking out for them, the dragons remained vulnerable: hunters would come across them in mountain passes and kill them out of fear, and fishermen would see them in lakes and rivers and destroy them out of competition. There came a day, not long ago at all, when the Uktena dragons became extinct, and all that remained were a handful of unhatched eggs in the secret possession of the queen.

"It was during the reign of this queen that Hernando de Soto sailed to Turtle Island. When he and his men arrived at her village, she was taken prisoner, and all her belongings stolen. When de Soto came upon the eggs, he mistook them for pearls and tried to take them as well, but the queen erupted in such anger that he allowed her to retain them, just to keep her happy so that she would be a cooperative hostage and secure his men food and shelter from the tribes they passed as they continued their invasion. But the queen was far smarter than the Spaniards believed, and one day she made her escape, taking the eggs with her. De Soto was distraught, as he had planned to steal the pearls from her anyway when he no longer needed her help.

"The eggs have been in South Carolina ever since, still guarded night and day by the ancient woman's line. None but the current guardian knows exactly where they are, and no one but her daughter ever will."

"So they're not extinct, then," Eilwen exclaimed as soon as she sensed the story was over. She couldn't seem to help herself. "The eggs could still hatch. Couldn't they?"

"They're over five hundred years old," said Conor. "If they're not dead now, they were likely never alive to begin with. Duds."

"One did hatch recently," Ayasta corrected, then shrugged and returned to studying the reflection of the moon in the pond. "Nothing survived, but it did hatch. The anniversary is coming up. That's why the adults are so uneasy."

"Are they that sad about a baby Uktena?" Eilwen asked.

"It's more than that," said Conor. "The anniversary of the egg dying is also the anniversary of the Uktena Child. They happened on the same night. There are witches in South Carolina who blame New Salem for the death of that egg."

"Why? And what is the Uktena Child?" Eilwen turned to Ayasta. "You mentioned that the day you and Ivy met me."

"The Uktena Child was a witch born here in New Salem some years back who had an enemy who wanted to kill her so badly that the Border was nearly successfully penetrated." Conor's voice was a monotone, yet somehow ripe with concern.

Ayasta was calm when she corrected, "It *was* successfully penetrated. Only for a second or two. But long enough to damage the infant and mother. Both died that night. It was the first time in history an enemy was able to reach us from the outside. It rattles many who remember it. It made us feel vulnerable in our own homes for the first time in our lives."

"What's that got to do with an Uktena?" asked Eilwen confusedly.

"You remember I told ya Sacred Bundles are only used in dire emergencies? The Bundles are so dangerously powerful because they contain living pieces of Uktena. That's what Ayasta meant when she said Uktena magic was used to create the Border."

"*Living* pieces?"

"Flesh that somehow never rots. Blood that never congeals. Scales and skin that never decay. Ancient, potent magic that not even the oldest shamans fully comprehend," said Ayasta. "The most powerful Bundles – like the one in my coven – contain an *Ulun'suti*: a shining, crystal stone that once rested on the dragons' foreheads, between their eyes. It was the most powerful part of the Great Serpent. It's said that when Uktena went to the sky's edge, she stole a piece of the Sun and brought it back with her, and wore it proudly on her head for the rest of her life. All her children hatched with the sun between their eyes, and hunters sought the jewel for its beauty and power. Even after an Uktena was killed, that third eye remained aware and living.

"My coven's Bundle was consulted the night the Border was attacked. It resealed the Border and strengthened its protective power. But the damage had been done to the infant witch and her mother. Both were dying. The Bundle was consulted again to try and save them, but since the magic that had attacked them had been powerful enough to break the Border, their bodies could not recover. The mother died first. A Welshwoman, I believe. Fled her home to escape whatever evil followed her here. The baby survived some time, thanks to the Bundle, but she died that night as well. The next day, reports from

South Carolina spread across the country that one of the last Uktena eggs had mysteriously disappeared – simply died and dissolved, for no reason, despite surviving centuries of dormancy. Many choose to believe it hatched, and that the infant dragon didn't survive either. So we call the dead infant witch *Uktena Child*, and recall her to ground us and remind us we are not invulnerable."

"When my mother first met you, she was convinced you were the Uktena Child," Conor said to Eilwen. "That the infant witch had somehow survived. You would have both been the same age. And you're an orphan with a Welsh name who was chosen by a snake. It all seemed too coincidental."

"I wasn't the Uktena Child, though, obviously," Eilwen laughed at the absurdity. "I was born in Bowling Green. Besides, you told me Mona wasn't lying that day in town. That I was every bit as much her niece as Gus was her nephew."

Conor shrugged. "Auras don't lie, and your aunt weren't lying. Doesn't mean it all ain't one hell of a coincidence, though."

* * *

At one point in the night, Eilwen, Conor, Ayasta and Ivy were all approached in their spot beneath the oak tree by a small group of witches about their age. Eilwen was still reeling from the Uktena stories and so barely noticed when Ivy said her name. Ivy nudged her, and, having Eilwen's attention, nodded toward the approaching witches.

233

"That's Epona Nolan," Ivy explained, indicating a pretty Fire witch who appeared to be the leader of the group. Eilwen recognized her as the young witch who had been at Priestess Reagan's side earlier. "Epona, Reagan, Conor, Ygraine, and Arden are five of only nine Fires in all Kentucky. Epona's being groomed to be High Priestess one day. Only Fires can hold that position. That's why covens are so protective of Fires when they have them."

"Ivy still feels bad about shooting you and is trying to rationalize it," Ayasta summarized dryly, and choked on her food when Ivy shoved her.

Eilwen noticed Conor had gone very quiet.

"How come Conor isn't being groomed for that position?" she asked.

"I'm a warlock." Conor sounded bitter.

When Eilwen looked puzzled, Ayasta explained, "Magic is stronger in women than in men." (Eilwen heard Conor try and fail to hold back a snort.) "A coven would sooner give a powerful position to an Air witch than to a Fire warlock."

"But that's not fair," said Eilwen. "Conor's powerful! What's his being a boy got to do with whether he'd make a good leader?"

"Well, everything." Ayasta sounded surprised she even had to explain this. "Warlocks just don't have what it takes."

"We could," snapped Conor, "if we weren't all raised in a matriarchal culture doin' everything in its power to keep men from being —"

"Yeah, Conor, we're heard it all before," Ivy sighed dismissively, and Conor's eyes flared. "Warlocks are victims of social bias!" Ivy continued sarcastically. "Life's not fair! You're *so* deprived! *Puh.* To hear you talk, you'd think witches keep warlocks chained in stockades all day."

"Look, I agree warlocks aren't given proper representation in coven politics," Ayasta intervened diplomatically, for Conor looked retaliatory, "but Conor, you have to admit witches are just more powerful. We're born with that advantage. It's nature. Even other warlocks acknowledge and accept it."

"And they're part of the problem," Conor retorted.

"Is this the political difference Ygraine has?" Eilwen asked Conor quietly.

He was about to answer but Epona and her following had reached them.

Eilwen could see the resemblance between Epona and her mother right away, particularly in the way Epona's eyes strayed automatically to Eilwen. She and Reagan also shared the same tight curls of auburn hair and hazel-brown eyes. They even both carried themselves with the same queen-like demeanor. Epona's robes were light pink, stitched with swirling red flames and stars. The four witches devotedly following her were green-eyed, all born to Earth; Eilwen got the impression that in the absence of fellow Fire witches, Epona surrounded herself instead with members of the second rarest Element available.

"We weren't expecting Ygraine to grace us with her presence this evening." Epona, now ignoring Eilwen altogether, bowed her head ever so slightly as she greeted Conor.

"She is a might unpredictable." Conor barely acknowledged her in return.

"She's so concerned about your new houseguest joining us," Epona continued nonetheless, sounding almost angered. "Does that mean she's having a change of heart about leaving herself?"

"Ask her. She's right over there, avoiding your mother."

Epona's face was unreadable. She tucked a curl behind her ear and lifted an eyebrow. Eilwen wondered suddenly if this sort of clash was what happened when two people used to being praised for their rarity were forced to interact.

Was this some tradition? Fires having to greet and acknowledge each other? Conor did not seem to care for Epona, and Epona did not seem particularly pleased to see him either. Eilwen thought she saw her eyes flash in her direction again before locking once more on Conor's purposefully indifferent face.

"Well, I just hope that since you're fighting so hard for your friend to join us, you plan on staying a good long while yourself." She grinned tightly and tipped her head before turning to leave. As she did, she caught Eilwen's eye and sneered at her.

Eilwen, utterly taken aback, widened her eyes. When Epona and her friends had gone, Eilwen looked at Ivy and Ayasta to see if they were as shocked as she was. They didn't seem to be.

"Did I... do something?" she asked unsurely.

"Not a thing." Ayasta sounded reassuringly firm, as though expecting Eilwen's question. "Not a single thing. Please don't fret, Eilwen."

Ivy handed Eilwen one of the tarts she'd been eating.

But it was Epona's final words that bothered Eilwen once they registered. "Do you not plan on staying in the coven, Conor?"

Conor took a long, deep breath, as though he had to finally face some awful, uncomfortable truth he'd been hoping beyond hope to be able to avoid. "I'm part of the coven until I turn twenty-one," he said simply, never looking at her.

Eilwen gawked at him, not even trying to hide her worry. "What happens when you turn twenty-one?"

"I'll be of age. And I'll have to either perform the duties allotted to me by the coven or leave altogether, like my mother did."

"Is that why she left? She didn't want to perform her duties?" That didn't sound like Ygraine.

"She didn't agree with the duties," Conor clarified.

"What were they?"

"To let the coven... do what they wanted with me. Fires are rare, so when one is born, there are particular laws that apply to us. Mostly to keep us safe. I'm one of only nine Fires in the state. And New Salem... well, they've a law that... when a Fire is born... if there's another Fire of similar age, and..."

Conor looked up at the sky, then clasped his hands and looked down, biting his lip. Finally, he raised his head level and stared directly ahead, expressionless, and Eilwen thought she could feel his suffocation at having the right words escape. At long last, he stated, plainly and without the slightest inflection or intonation that could risk being misread in any way, "I'm engaged."

Eilwen's entire body went numb. Her throat constricted. Somehow her heart seemed to burn and freeze at the same time. She had to speak lowly to keep her voice from cracking when she asked, "To who?" Though she did not know why she asked: she already knew the answer.

"Epona." Conor still would not look at her.

Eilwen felt as though her heart had dropped into her stomach. She looked over across the fire pit and studied the girl in the pink-and-red-flamed gown. Suddenly, Eilwen completely understood Conor's disdain for Dristan.

Ayasta and Ivy remained silent. Neither said anything as Eilwen excused herself, stood, and walked away.

Conor still would not look at her.

* * *

Eilwen was crying against the side of a barn when Ayasta found her.

"I'm so sorry." She took Eilwen in her arms and sat with her. "It was cruel of him to lead you on. I warned him, weeks ago. And then I saw him dance with you tonight, and I knew he was the cruelest person I'd ever met. There's a saying, that the quickest way to get an Air witch to fall in love with you is to dance with her. Swirling like air currents to sound and music... There's no quicker way to catch one's heart. Especially if she already likes you. It was cruel of him, Eilwen. I'm so sorry."

Ayasta held her tightly, patted her gently, and whispered soothing things. Eilwen tried her hardest to stop crying, for she did not want Ayasta to feel her efforts to comfort were in vain. But she could not seem to stop. The tears kept flowing.

She was grateful she had calmed down by the time Ivy came to find them. Her eyes stung and tears still rolled down her face, but the worst was over when Ivy said, "Ygraine sent for you, Eilwen. She and Conor are ready to go home."

Ayasta and Ivy walked supportively on either side of her as they returned to the fire pit. Eilwen almost cried again, this time from gratefulness. Was this what friendship was?

The fire pit was nearly vacated. What few witches remained were huddled near the door of one of the cabins, arguing loudly with one another. Conor was standing off to the side, leaning against a tree with his arms crossed, glaring sideways at the conundrum. Ygraine was literally in the middle of it all.

"You must know *something* about this." Reagan sounded accusatory, but more fearful than anything. "Someone from your family? A distant relative from the Ireland Coven? The letter is signed with the name Sheehan! You must have some idea who this is from!"

The murmur grew louder. Múireann, the Water Priestess, was holding a folded letter that she handed over to Arden as soon as the High Priestess held out her hand.

"What does it say *exactly*?" demanded another witch. "The precise wording. Perhaps it doesn't mean what we think."

Arden held the letter in front of her and, in the same calm but powerful voice she'd commanded when speaking before the fire, read, "*The device still exists and I know who holds it.*"

The murmuring escalated again. Ygraine stood silently at Arden's side, her face as unreadable as Conor's had been before Eilwen had left him in tears.

"It is signed, *Fledyra Sheehan*," Arden finished, and turned to look at Ygraine.

Ygraine returned the High Priestess's gaze without flinching. "I tell you – and you know I tell you true, Arden MacNessa – that I've no earthly idea who such a person is."

"I do."

Eilwen felt herself stepping forward before she was even aware of what she was doing. Ayasta and Ivy blanched as the High Council and surrounding witches turned to look for who had spoken. Ygraine met Eilwen's eyes, and for the first time ever, Eilwen saw her appear confused. Shocked.

Arden silenced everyone. Eilwen trembled under her stare.

"Fledyra Sheehan," Arden repeated. "Young tobacco farmer, you claim you know whose name this is?"

Eilwen swallowed and nodded.

"I do," she said. "It's my mother's name."

Eilwen's story will continue in the next book in the series.

About the author:

Gwen Kaelin is a young woman who lives with her mother, father, and little sister in Louisville, Kentucky, where she was born and raised. She wrote the first chapters of Eilwen when she was thirteen years old, and has dreamed of being an author since she was even younger. Her hobbies are writing, reading, daydreaming, drawing, playing piano, taking walks through nature, and watching TV with her dogs, cats, and snake.

Visit www.gwenkaelin.com for updates on when new books will be released.